Honolulu Story

HONOLULU STORY

HONOLULU STORY

By

LESLIE FORD

WILDSIDE PRESS

Honolulu Story

Published by Wildside Press LLC
www.wildsidepress.com

WITH ALOHA

Harold Standiford, *Seaman 1st Class* USN

Howard L. Cantz, *Cpl.* USMC

William P. Ervin, *Pvt.* USMC

Richard E. Oly, *Pfc.* USMC

Paul E. Swain, *Pfc.* USMCR

HONOLULU STORY

1

NIGHT LAY LIKE A CLOAK OF SABLE FEATHERS, silver-bordered where the quiet rollers of the Pacific broke on the outlying coral reef and broke again as they swept up the long concave line of the shallow beach.

The boy stood motionless by a wind-stunted clump of kiave trees in the dunes, his rifle in one hand, his dog held hard on the leash with the other. His eyes, trained to darkness and the deceptive shimmer of shifting starlight, picked out the rock that when the spray subsided for a moment on the reef looked like a swimmer poised to dive. He looked slowly over the inlet to the empty beach, across the narrow plateau, arid, sparsely grown with the kiave, and up at the black volcanic rock towering in a sheer palisade above him.

Every other night of his solitary patrol along the beach he had looked up at the mountain fortress stretching the whole length of the Island and thought of it as he did in the daytime—a grim barren wall that cut off the windward side of Oahu from Honolulu, shutting him off from the only civilized spot on the God-forsaken dump . . . the Rock, the GI's called it, and the missionaries could have it back tomorrow. But tonight it was, different. It was closer to him, higher, more densely black and impenetrable, brooding, powerful and alive.

He moved sharply and the dog stiffened and strained forward. But there was nothing on the beach. He was just jittery.

He thought about it, looking up into the black wall of silence again. The Hawaiian girl had begged him and the other boy from camp not to go into the burial cave. They wouldn't have gone, maybe, if she hadn't been so frightened. It was funny, too. They had been all over there a dozen times when there wasn't anything to do at camp. It was funny they hadn't seen the mouth of the cave before. It wasn't big but it was hard to see how anybody could have missed it. This morning it was right out in plain sight when they climbed up the ledge to pick some ground orchids for the girl. It almost looked as if they were supposed to find it.

His body went taut again, and the dog, responding instantly, strained on the leash, silent and alert. Again it was nothing, just the wind in the kiave. It wasn't the music of the People they said came singing out of the mist at night, or the distant beating of drums he'd read about being heard in the hills.

The burial caves were like that too. Only one person was allowed to know where any one was buried, and he handed the secret down to one other in sacred trust when he knew, as Hawaiians seemed to know, when death was coming to him. Even the burial place of Kamehameha the Great, whose statue was everywhere, had never been found, and no one knew who the guardian of his secret was.

The girl's pale frightened face seemed to come to him out of the mountain wall, her great liquid brown eyes imploring them not to go into the cave. He could hear her frantic words telling them the terrible things that had happened to other people, and hear their laughter echoing back as they wriggled in on their stomach, and the sudden silence when they were inside. The air was heavy and their GI lighters kept going out. They had crouched down and felt around on the ground. He had found a long bone, the other boy a calabash. Then they couldn't find their way out again. The sweat stood out on the sentry's forehead as he remembered that silent panic, and the dog quivered on the leash. When they had found the way at last the girl was gone. They had stopped at her house, on a back road on the way to camp, but the house was locked and barred and the blinds pulled down. Not even a dog came out to meet them. It gave them a funny kind of feeling that they felt again as an old Hawaiian up the road shrank out of their path, mumbling quickly to himself, his eyes tightly closed, as if the curse was already visible in their faces.

He still had the bone, and the other boy the calabash he'd broken when he slipped coming down the ledge. He wanted to throw the bone away but he didn't want the other boy to think he was afraid. And it was the other boy the car hit when they crossed the road to camp. That was funny too, because the road was empty and the car in plain sight.

He shook himself a little and tightened his grip on the leash. The solid wall of the great mountain seemed to loom closer and blacker, and the flesh along his spine prickled cold and hot. The dog jerked abruptly. He looked away from the mountain out to the reef. His hands were trembling and the wind was like fingers crawling across his face. If he could only light a cigarette, he thought. There was no use patrolling the beach any more, anyway. Nothing would come. The Japs were licked—they needed all the submarines they had closer home. He fixed his eyes on the reef where the spray subsiding left the rock that looked like a swimmer about to dive. That was something he was sure of. Then, as he looked, he knew he was not sure of anything any more.

The rock jutting up looked wider. It looked as if it were moving too, like the mountain wall moving closer. He closed his eyes quickly, gripping his rifle tighter, gripping the leash. When he looked again he took a long breath. It was just an illusion. The rock was solid again and motionless as the spray came up around it, blotting it out.

He turned abruptly and started along the beach. The dog held back, bristling.

"Don't be a dope," the boy said aloud. "Come on.

It's just a ghost trying to get his shin bone back."

As he said it there was something, a sound, behind him, and for the first time on his patrol of the lonely beach he knew fear, so strong that he knew he was afraid to turn around. For an instant it paralyzed his feet and held his heart frozen as it tingled like drops of molten steel down his spine and poured cold sweat out of every pore in his body. Then he turned suddenly, to face it, and there was nothing there . . . nothing but the empty beach, the breaking waves, the kiave on the wind-swept dunes under the black fortress of the Kuloo Range, and the dog, straining, quivering, on the leash.

His own body went taut, his heart pounded, alive again. He leaned forward quickly and unleashed the dog. The lean black body flashed as it leaped forward, silent as a savage arrow, to where the slithering sound had come from the trees. The boy's finger was steady on the cold trigger of his rifle as he crept forward, holding his breath. The cave of the secret dead was forgotten, and the boy with the broken calabash. The mountain receded and diminished. He waited, tense and coordinated and sane again, and crept forward, crouching low. He could see the dog's tracks, crossing the beach through the dunes to the narrow concrete road. He ran to the road, crouched lower still as he crossed it, and stopped.

The sand was wet there. He looked down at it, back at the road, across the beach to the edge of the ocean and out to the reef where the solid black column jutted up, the swimmer about to dive. He lay there silently, listening, crouched low to the ground. There was no answer to his low call to the dog, nothing but the wind in the dry trees, and the muted roll of waves breaking on the reef and whispering along the shallow beach.

He crept forward, tense, under the black fortress of the mountain. He should go back and report, he knew, but if he could get the man . . . ? If there was a man, he thought . . . a man of flesh and blood. . . . The dark swift shadow behind him moved almost noiselessly. The boy turned too late even to see the white ghost's face and the flashing gleam of the naked blade. . . .

They found him there very early in the morning, staring sightlessly up at the dark empty sky. The dog lay at the bottom of a rock, his throat slashed open. It was still before dawn when the young officer came back with the thick-set, gray-haired colonel.

"Thought you'd want to see this, Colonel Primrose," he said. "I've got orders to keep you informed. This isn't the man you're after, though. It looks like a dirty Jap to me. White men don't use a knife this way."

The man he spoke to, standing in front of the huge sergeant, looked down, his black eyes softening for an instant, at the dead boy's body. He looked back to where the single track of footprints, too solidly indented to be a ghost's, came up the lonely beach out of the Pacific Ocean. He looked up at the black volcanic rock. No one had ever charted the hidden caves formed in the gigantic turmoil that thousands of years ago threw up the floor of the ocean in masses of molten lava to make the islands and atolls of the Pacific. Somewhere up there, in a cave, or beyond, invisible in the growth of bush and vine and tree that stretched into a wilderness of jungle, was the man who had crept silently up out of the midnight sea. Unless, Colonel John Primrose thought, he had already found his friends. . . .

Colonel Primrose's black eyes hardened as he looked down again at the dead boy.

"Perhaps," he said quietly. "We'll find out."

2

THE THIRD TIME TOMMY DAWSON SAID, "JEEP-ers, it's time for us to go home," I realized it was double talk, and not meant for himself alone of the three boys there. The only move he'd made when he said it was forward in his chair a little until some gal with bare brown arms and legs and a red or yellow hibiscus in her black hair had passed along the street out of sight of his roving eyes.

The four of us—Tommy Dawson, Dave Boyer, Swede Ellicott and I—were sitting in the broad open lounge of the Moana Hotel in Waikiki. The three of them were lieutenants in the Army Air Force, back from the Marianas for ten days' rest. And I thought, at the time, that I was Grace Latham, just arrived in Honolulu from Washington, D. C., on what they call "invitational orders." They seemed important and even impressive the day they were issued, but they were a snare and a delusion, as perhaps I should have realized before I heard any one else say so. It's clear to me now that what I actually was was nothing other than a plain booby-trap, the brain child of my old friend Colonel

John Primrose, 92nd Engineers U. S. Army (Retired) and acting special agent in Military Intelligence. And no doubt it's the chief reason why Colonel Primrose's guard, philosopher and friend, and self-styled "functotum," Sergeant Phineas T. Buck, doesn't really have to worry—dreadfully though he does—about his colonel's ever marrying me. He'd have to find another lady fall guy if he did.

Tommy Dawson craned his red head forward again. *"Baby!"*

Dave Boyer growled irritably.

"Oh, shut up. For cripe's sake lay off, can't you?"

His sensitive sun-blackened face went a shade darker and his mouth tightened. Of the three he was the only one who looked as if he really needed the rest he'd been sent back to get. The casual way he sat there was deceptive, but his finger nails were chewed down to the quick. Twice Tommy Dawson had stuck a foot out, given him a quiet nudge and said, "Hi, boy," and I'd seen the hunted shadow in his brown eyes disappear as he'd raised his thumb and forefinger in a circle with a quick "Okay, thanks." But he was sore now.

"Just lay off," he said. "For about ten seconds."

Tommy Dawson lay back in his chair, grinning.

"Why, David," he said. "My dear old friend and brother officer, don't get me wrong. All I'm saying is, I can't take it. I just can't take lolling here in this whispering paradise of sunlight and palm trees. It's sapping my fiery determination to win the Pacific war single-handed. Listen to the sapphire wavelets caressing the silver strand. Listen to the haunting melody of romance floating through the tender moonlit stillness———"

"Just shut up, is all I said."

The only haunting melody of romance audible at the moment was coming from the juke box across the streaming Sunday afternoon madhouse of Kalakaua Avenue, and it was all but drowned out by the jeeps and taxis and buses and the shrill congress of mynah birds in the palm tree outside. The wide street, glaring white in the intense clarity of the afternoon sunlight, was a swarm of sailors and seabees, soldiers and marines. A few of them were with girls—Waves, Wacs and the little lady Marines in their bright green and scarlet and white. A few were with the civilian girls with bare brown arms and legs and red or yellow hibiscus in their coal-black hair. Most of them hunted singly or in packs. They jammed the curio shops with the grass skirts in the windows. They stood endlessly in line for food or a movie or a bus to take them somewhere to stand in other lines for food or a movie or a bus to take them somewhere else, wishing to a man they were back at the corner drug store on Main Street.

To our left across the lounge, the line to the dining room already stretched half the length of the lanai. GI's and sailors, officers and men and an occasional civilian, stood drearily inching forward, paying no attention to the sapphire wavelets on the famous beach

at Waikiki. It was just at the end of the crowded courtyard, within what Sergeant Buck would have called
spitting distance and could easily have proved it. The
silver strand was hardly visible for sun-tanned bodies,
but beyond it were thousands of blue miles of ocean,
as calm as an inland lake except where the long low
rollers broke for an instant in great white feathers on
the coral reef. Surfboards and a few outrigger canoes
gave it a slight touch of the tourist ads, a semi-tropical
Coney Island, but chiefly the whole scene was like a
cross between the Grand Central Station and Market
Street when the Fleet's in.

Tommy Dawson's hair was red, his face freckled,
and he had in him what Lilac, who's my cook and friend
in my house on P Street in Georgetown, District of
Columbia, calls a devil as big as a house.

"*Jeepers!*" he said again.

Dave Boyer's lean body moved.

"—Relax, David. Just relax."

Swede Ellicott reached a long leisurely arm out of
the deep wicker chair beside Tommy and knocked the
dottle out of his pipe into the ash stand between them.
He was big and blond and unhurried. The Central
Pacific had bleached his eyebrows so they looked like
thick patches of straw above his light blue eyes. His
face was burned and weather-beaten, not handsome and
in fact far from it, and curiously ingenuous, I thought,
for anything so rugged and hard-bitten. He had the
casual matter-of-fact air that seems to be as much a

part of a flyer's uniform as the dog-eared nonchalance of his cap.

"Don't pay him no mind, David," he said placidly. "I'm deaf. I ain't heard nothin' he been sayin'.—Hullo, they must be looking for somebody."

He pointed out the window. I saw two small planes that looked like white birds flying very low against the back drop of the mountain range above the city. They were moving so slowly that they looked stationary until they banked and wheeled back, mounting a little higher each time until they were against the blue sky.

We had all bent down and looked at them, and we were all silent for a moment, watching them. I can believe, now, that we were each aware of some subtle kind of premonitory warning, coming maybe out of the deep substratum of primitive mysticism that's lingered on in the Hawaiian atmosphere in spite of the missionaries and in spite of modern science. I don't insist on it, but we were silent, for a moment, watching those searching planes, and no one else seemed to be interested, and it was the four of us, of all the people there in the Moana lobby or on the street, who were to be caught up and vitally affected . . . Swede Ellicott, who'd noticed them first and commented on them, the most vitally and fundamentally of us all.

Maybe, of course, it was only because Swede and the other two were just back from an area where it's important to be acutely conscious of any plane that's acting in an unusual fashion. But there were other flyers just back too, not even aware of the two white ships, searching, against the hills and the sky. And we dismissed them at once, rejecting the warning if it was a warning. We'd not heard then that a sentry had been killed on the other side of the Island, or that a man had come up out of the Pacific Ocean who had forfeited every right of God or man to set his foot ever again on Hawaii nei so long as he lived. Nor did we recognize, a very few minutes later, in what appeared to be a purely personal matter between the three boys and a girl, another stone in the bridge already building that would reach, when it was finished, far across the grim valley where death sits, waiting.

Swede Ellicott turned back to me.

"How's Washington, Grace? And how's the ancient and honorable, my aunt?"

Up to that point none of the three had so much as mentioned Washington, not even in asking what kind of a flight I'd had and when I started on it. Since it was in Washington I'd seen them last, and had met them in the first place, when the three of them and a boy named Ben Farrell were keeping what is sometimes called bachelor hall at Swede's aunt's place next door to mine, I'd assumed they were avoiding the whole subject with reason. I was avoiding it with what I thought was tact.

The reason was a girl named Mary Cather. The tact was because I'd never been very sure as to what had happened. I knew they'd all been in love with her and that Swede Ellicott had been engaged to marry her. It was one of those things that happen with the speed and brilliance of light, for Swede and Mary. The enchantment she wore like a star in her shining gold hair that night wasn't visible to me, but it was devastating magic to the three young men who'd just got their wings, and to Ben Farrell newly commissioned in the Marine Corps. It wasn't a full two days later before Swede told me they were going to be married. Right away, he said, but I knew Mary's mother would see to that, and probably Swede's aunt, because Mary was a stranger in Washington. She was there with her mother as a reluctant evacuée from the bombing of Pearl Harbor, resenting it silently but bitterly. That may, of course, have been part of the magic glamor she had for the four boys that night. It was definitely part of the situation there that moment when we were sitting in the lobby of the Moana Hotel, because Mary Cather was back in Honolulu.

Her engagement to Swede hadn't lasted very long. It was about three months, in fact, from the night they met at my house, that Mrs. Cather called on me and told me it was broken. She didn't say why, except that Swede had acted very badly. She also said Mary was being very difficult. It had been too sudden to last, anyway, she thought, and she'd been opposed to it from the beginning—which I think was not quite correct. She was genuinely disturbed about Mary, there was no doubt of that, though why again she didn't say. Chiefly what she said was she was determined their paths should not cross again. If I ever heard from Swede's aunt next door that Swede was coming back, she wanted me to let her know so she could take Mary to New York until he left. She didn't want them ever to meet again. Swede's aunt, on the other hand, a very rigid Washington cave-dweller of the old and almost extinct species, maintained a tight-lipped silence about the whole thing, including Swede, even when I asked her how and where he was.

So it was a peculiarly ironic full turn of the wheel for Swede Ellicott to be here in Honolulu when Mary had just returned from the Mainland, their paths converging at the crossroads of the Pacific. Whether they were going to do more than converge and actually cross was in a sense in my hands just then . . . and I'd been thinking about it, not too happily, ever since I'd taken down the phone that afternoon and heard Swede's voice at the other end. All three of them had avoided mentioning Mary Cather, but I wasn't sure that now they'd got around to Washington and Swede's aunt they wouldn't get around to her.

"Washington's fine," I said. I went on for a moment about the ghastly winter and about Swede's aunt. Then I stopped, aware that neither he nor either of the other two was hearing a word I was saying. None of them had moved, but their attention was fixed, intense and concentrated, out of the open window. There was a curious light in Swede's eyes that neither of the others

had. All three of them were staring at a girl coming
quickly along, out there, through a barrage of quite
uninhibited public admiration.

I glanced back at Tommy Dawson, expecting to hear
a really heartfelt "Jeepers!" this time. The girl didn't
have a hibiscus in her hair, but she had a carnation lei
around her neck and she was certainly the type. She
had dark, almond-shaped eyes and high, full checkbones
and her lips were very red, and she came through the
uniformed stag line that opened and formed again behind her with the smiling assurance of a veteran, slim
and lithe and quite unabashed. But Tommy Dawson
was silent, his lips tight. Dave Boyer's eyes burned with
a sharp antagonism that he looked down abruptly to
conceal.

Swede Ellicott took one foot down slowly from the
sofa, then the other, and got up, not looking at either
of them.

"Well," he said, "I've got to shove." He put on his
cap and pulled it down in back. "Nice seeing you, Mrs.
Latham. I'll give you a call. So long. So long, you
guys."

"So long," Tommy said. It was clipped off so short
that Swede hesitated an instant. He turned and made
his way deliberately across the lounge and toward the
main entrance and the girl with the carnation lei.

It wasn't hard to see where she was. Being a woman
in a practically womanless hotel lobby she was where
everybody was looking. Even the men waiting with
duffel bags and blue and khaki canvas gripsacks at the

elevator brightened up and looked as long as she was alone. As she spotted Swede Ellicott all heads turned in unison to look at him. It was a curious pantomime, and so was her meeting with Swede. It was obviously prearranged and she was perfectly aware of Tommy Dawson and Dave Boyer in our corner. She glanced over and turned back, laughing up at Swede. He didn't look around, not even when they got into a taxi outside and passed directly by the open window where we were sitting, the silence between the two men about as grim as silence can be.

I was silent too. Any idea I'd had of mentioning Mary Cather I decided to put quietly away until I knew what was going on. Where Swede Ellicott's interest was at the moment was all too clear, and something I would never for an instant have thought of. The fact that Tommy and Dave were taking it as they did was a relief to me. I'd have hated to think I was shocked at anything they would take for granted.

When Dave Boyer spoke his voice was abrupt and bitter, and he had to make an effort to keep it steady.

"I *told* you to lay off."

"Nuts," Tommy said. "She's got him hooked. He hasn't got a prayer—not a whisper. I wish to——"

He turned to look at Dave and stopped.

"Steady!" he said quietly. "Come on—take it easy, boy. Come on, David—snap!"

Dave Boyer was quite white and his hands holding his pipe were shaking.

"She hasn't got him," he whispered. "It's not going

to happen—not again. She's not going to marry Swede."
His voice rose. "By God I'll kill her first."

"—Easy, boy."

I don't suppose I actually repeated the words "marry Swede," but they were certainly framed on my lips. I couldn't believe I'd heard them. It wasn't possible. Swede Ellicott must be out of his mind to think of marrying a girl . . . I hesitated. I knew nothing about her, only that regardless of everything else she was of an alien race. I looked blankly at the two boys.

Tommy Dawson glanced around us. The strangled intensity of Dave Boyer's voice had carrying power. Only the mynah birds and the traffic and the general din of too many people in too small a space had kept what he'd said from being a public declaration.

"—I wouldn't," he said quietly. "It isn't Corinne's fault. She'd never have got to first base by herself. It's that she-buzzard in Washington."

It hardly seemed to me the way to speak of my next door neighbor, though I did have a sneaking feeling there was something to be said for the point of view. But inasmuch as Swede had at least politely referred to her as the ancient and honorable his aunt, I couldn't see what she had to do with the situation this far out in the Pacific. She would certainly be the last person in the world to approve of the girl with the carnation lei.

Dave Boyer looked at him. "You're right," he said slowly. "You're right."

Tommy Dawson pulled in his long legs and got up. "I guess I was right in more ways than one," he said. "I guess it's time for us to go home too. There's a bus pretty soon. Come on, David."

He put out a sunburned freckled hand.

"That's the only thing we've ever held against you, lady," he said. "We were four happy Joes—calabash brothers, they call 'em here—till you brought the little Cather into our lives. And the little Cather's ma. It was a lousy deal, lady. Now one of us is dead on her account, and the big Swede . . ."

He tried to grin.

"Well, the big Swede wouldn't have been a pushover for this babe you just saw if your friend Mrs. Cather hadn't pulled a fast one the minute he got his back turned. That's how she got poor old Ben. We're damned if she's going to marry the Swede too. So . . . the big Swede's on your head—do what you can, will you?"

He dropped my hand and turned to pick up his cap. "Come on, David. Let's shove. Let's get the hell out. Let's get the hell back to Saipan. . . ."

I sat there for several minutes simply staring after them, upset and shaken. Ben Farrell, the fourth of what they'd called the Organization when they came to batch next door to me, was dead, and he'd been married to the half-Japanese girl. And it wasn't Swede's aunt they were calling a she-buzzard. It was Alice Cather . . . the little Cather's ma. The whole thing was incredible. Above all, how either Mary or her mother could be responsible for either Ben's death or his marriage, was more than I could conceive. Or how they could call Alice Cather what they had, for that matter. If Alice was a she-buzzard she was also a genius at camouflage. I didn't know her intimately, but I did know her well enough to know that much. Between her saying Swede had behaved very badly and Tommy's obviously sincere conviction that both she and Mary had behaved worse, I was stranded on an unhappy and bewildering middle ground. I was very glad indeed that I hadn't told Tommy or Dave—or Swede—that the two of them, Mary and her mother, were there in Honolulu, or that as soon as they left I was going to the Cathers' to have dinner and spend the night.

3

I KEPT TRYING TO FIGURE SOME SENSE OUT of it as I waited for the major who was to come and take me to the Cathers' house. They lived up the Pali road. To any one who thinks, as I did, of the Hawaiian Islands as a vast semitropical beach with girls in grass skirts dotting sunlit pineapple and cane fields, it's a shock to find mountains everywhere. Honolulu spills into the sea out of a broad lee-side valley below folding hills, like the end of a great cornucopia made by two wild volcanic ranges. The whole windward side of the Island is a vast precipice above a narrow seaside plain and is called the pali, which means precipice. What is called the Pali is a sheer staggering drop of twelve hundred feet where there's a narrow pass over the Koolu Range up Nuuanu Avenue from the swarming city. Because it's the most dramatic place on the Island and I hadn't been up there yet and we were early, my escort and I passed the Cathers' entrance on the winding tropical road and went on up to see it.

I don't bring this in because I'm writing a guide for the post-war tourist, but for two other reasons. The first is that when we got back into the car out of the tearing wind and sat a moment looking out over the narrow plain below us, it seemed to me there was an awful lot of deserted beach and rock-piled lonely coastline that was very vulnerable from the sea. And I'd been wondering about that.

"What's to keep a submarine from landing people along there at night?" I asked. I knew we'd landed people from submarines ourselves. It wasn't even necessary to surface to do it—they could be launched up from a hundred feet below if necessary.

The major looked at me a little oddly for just an instant. It was the sort of look I recognized from Washington, that's followed by a more or less polite evasion or some slightly sententious humor. But this was not being taken humorously, and I was aware suddenly that however far from the forward area the Islands might at present be, they were a lot farther forward than Washington.

"May I take that back?" I asked quickly.

"Not at all. We used to have barbed wire along the beaches. There's not much point in the Japs sending people in now. We still have patrols."

He switched the motor on and turned the car back toward the Cathers', and we went down in a rather sober silence.

The second reason I mention the Pali is that if I hadn't been lashed to bits by the trade wind whipping across the platform up there, I wouldn't have heard the redbird from the lanai outside Alice Cather's sitting room. I suppose the view of the windward side of the Island, with its rocky steeps and the narrow plain sloping down in the evening light to an indigo sea, was both magnificent and enchanting, but I was such a battered wreck trying to keep my skirt, my hair and the plumeria lei the major had bestowed on me in their proper places that I wasn't very appreciative.

The Cathers' courtyard as we drove in was full of cars, most of them bearing star-studded plates on the bumper. A Japanese house man in a starched white coat took my bags from the car, and Alice Cather at the door gave me one look.

"You've been up to the Pali. Come with me, dear—you look awful."

We went to the right along a passage away from the main quarters of the rambling house.

"I'll wait for you here."

She opened the door of her bedroom off a small sitting room that opened onto a lanai extending all around the house except at the entrance courtyard. "Your room's over there, but it isn't ready yet. You can get settled later."

Where we came in, the house was one long low story. Here it was high above the slope of the hill, with a swimming pool below and gardens that ended abruptly in what looked like a minor pali itself before it rose up farther along, steep and heavily wooded, into a mountain against the solid cobalt sky. It was wild, rugged and silent, totally unrelated to the seething madhouse that surrounded the beach of Waikiki, which could have been a thousand miles away and in another country.

"It's extraordinary, isn't it?" I said.

Alice Cather turned and looked at me as if she'd forgotten I was there and was surprised to see me.

"Oh," she said. "Yes. It is, isn't it?"

She was standing with her fingertips resting on the redwood rail, slight and straight as an arrow, with gray eyes and light graying hair, exquisitely groomed, with delicate and what I think are called patrician features. Her manner was patrician certainly, gracious and charming with so firmly lacquered a surface that it was impossible to know what kind of a woman was actually inside it. Up to then I'd never been interested in finding out. I was, now, seeing her against her own background for the first time. And still being concerned with what Tommy Dawson had said with too much sincerity to brush lightly aside, I decided if he was right it was time I knew it.

"It's quite extraordinary," she repeated.

We turned to go back. There was a fireplace in the wall in front of us, and over it the portrait of a man. It was fairly modern and strikingly done. The man who had sat was striking too. He had large luminous dark eyes in a fine, sensitive face. He was lean to the point of thinness, and the way his dark hair clung to his skull, and the line of his long hands resting on the arm of his chair, gave him a peculiarly gentle and patient expression.

"That's very nice," I said. "Is it your husband?"

I stopped to look at it, and Alice Cather stopped too.

"No," she said. "No. That isn't my husband. It's his brother."

She laughed lightly.

"I don't know why I said that. We let it go as my husband. Even Mary thinks it is. It was done when she was quite small, of course."

"Were they twins?"

She shook her head.

"Just a strong family resemblance. Completely unlike in every other respect, I may say. But he's dead."

I thought for an instant she was going to add, "Fortunately," but she didn't. She was looking at it as if she hadn't really seen it for a long time.

"—A strange family," she said then. "Oh, God, how strange they are!"

It came out so suddenly, and with a sharp break as she drew her breath quickly in, that I was more than startled, as I think she was herself. She turned abruptly and went out on the lanai.

"I wish to God I'd never come back, Grace," she said. She made a sharp movement with her head as if trying to shake something out of it.

"Forgive me—I don't know what's got into me lately. I've been like this for . . . weeks, it seems to me. Even in Washington. I didn't want to come back, but Mary was so set on it. I kept thinking it was going to be the plane, but up there I didn't have it. I lost it till we landed. Now it's back and it's worse."

Her eyes moved restlessly over the side of the hills beyond the garden.

"If I were Hawaiian I'd know. They always know what's going to happen. But I don't. All I know is I feel as if something ghastly is just over my head. I can't stand it, Grace . . . I'll go jump over the Pali if it doesn't stop. I think I'm going mad. I——"

She broke off abruptly, listening, and her face went slowly the color of dead ashes. She put her hand out and touched my arm.

"Grace," she whispered. "What was that? Do you hear it?"

All I could hear was the liquid sliding note of a bird somewhere in the pale green of the kukui trees in the ravine. At home I would have said it was a redbird calling. I didn't know what it would be in these fantastic hills.

"What is it, Grace?" she whispered again.

"It sounds like a cardinal to me," I said.

She turned her head slowly. "Of course." She gave a sort of broken laugh. "How absurd of me. I'm *really* losing my mind."

Inside the door she stopped and looked at herself in the gilded mirror over a large mat-covered sofa. The color was seeping back into her face and her eyes weren't so almost colorlessly gray.

"I meant to tell you, my dear," she said casually. "You have to be awfully careful about makeup out here. The air is so clear rouge stands out horribly. It makes one look hard. Let's go in, shall we?"

She rested her arm lightly in mine. "It's *so* nice you're here."

I wondered. My doubts, grave from the moment I'd stepped out of the transport plane, five thousand miles from home, onto the blistering surface of Hickam Field, and trod a minute section of over eleven miles of continuous concrete runway where Army and Navy air stations merge into a vast maelstrom at this cross-roads of the world, were really serious now. Maybe Alice Cather was more Hawaiian than she thought, the shadowy primeval wilderness around her more potent than she knew. It was silent, now, the redbird's note stilled in the evening woods. Maybe it was the threatening emanations from Tommy Dawson and Dave Boyer that she was feeling, I thought, and the perilous proximity of the man she wanted her daughter never to meet again. And so far as I was concerned, none of them ever would meet—I was determined about that. Tommy and Dave could take their rest and go back to Saipan, Swede Ellicott could marry the glamorous Corinne and regret at leisure, for all of me, and neither Mary Cather nor her mother need ever know how close those paths had come to crossing again. It was all too involved and unhappy. I didn't want to be any part of it.

We came into the long room that opened out onto

the lanai looking over the treetops down to the city
sprawling at the edge of the Pacific. Alice Cather was
superbly herself again, cool and assured and liquidly
charming.

"Harry, my dear, this is the Grace Latham, Mary
and I have told you so much about."

There were many other people in the room—men in
uniform with stars on their shoulders, women who were
handsome—but Harry Cather in his rumpled white
linen suit, and his daughter Mary, were as dominating
as the great mass of torch ginger that was the only
decoration against the silver-panelled wood walls, and
as arresting as the two little Japanese maids, kimono-
clad, slipping in and out among the guests with trays
of cocktails and hors d'œuvres. They were standing
together in front of the fireplace at the side of the room.
It was easy to see how the portrait of his brother back
in the sitting room could pass for Harry Cather, except
that his hair was white now and he wasn't so thin. I
saw the same large luminous dark eyes, rather sad until
he smiled, and the same patient, kindly droop of the
shoulders. He was very tall. His mouth was not as full
or sensuous as the portrait's, and his hand taking mine
was warm and very friendly.

"How do you do, Grace," he said smiling. "We call
people by their first names, here in the Islands, and
I've heard about you, from my daughter."

He turned to smile down at her.

"I hope you're going to love it here, Mrs. Latham,"
Mary said.

Standing there by her father, she was very different
from the silent resentful child I'd first seen on the
dock in San Francisco in February of '42. And different
from what she'd been in Washington. Seeing her now
I could understand the magic she'd distilled, or the
four young men on their way to war had divined in
her, the night they fell as a man. She'd been attractive
enough then so I wasn't worried about getting her as a
blind date for them. She was lovely, now, and the light
in her violet eyes as she looked up at her father was
lovely too. It must have been the way she looked at
the four boys that night. Her hair was in short curls
the color of shiny ripe wheatstraw that made her look
younger than her twenty years and the long bob she
wore in Washington had done. The sun tan she'd already got since she came home was a glowing and
golden apricot against the slim whiteness of her long
dress and the shower of white butterfly orchids on her
shoulder. But it was the radiance in her eyes that made
her different. They were clear as the dawn, and if any
shadow had ever touched them it was gone, forgotten
in the rapt enchantment of being home. Of guile or
duplicity there was none. And I could hear Tommy
Dawson's voice again:

"We were four happy Joes—now one of us is dead
on her account. . . ."

Her mother was at my side again, and I was meeting the other guests, with names I'd read in victorious
communiqués from the South and Central Pacific, some

of whom I'd already met around Washington. It was when Alice Cather led me to the lime-yellow cushioned hikiee in the corner that my heart gave a short power-dive and didn't come up.

"Well, bless me!" a voice said. "It sure is a small world, isn't it? How do you do, Mrs. Latham—I bet you don't remember me."

A young officer rose briskly. I bet I did remember him. He was one of those brash young men whose name never fully registers but whose face is as familiar at large cocktail parties as an established caterer's number one old waiter. He was some sort of a friend of the four boys who had a brother in the State Department and landed in its sacred precincts himself for a brief stay before General Hershey's large figure loomed ominously somewhat nearer than the horizon. And there must be some Hawaiian in me too. I knew what was coming as clearly as if he'd already said it.

"Have you seen the old gang yet? They'll all be here, all except Ben Farrell. . . ."

Alice Cather's hand on my elbow contracted sharply. I didn't look at her, and I couldn't see Mary without definitely turning. And I couldn't stop the young man.

"Poor old Ben got it, Saipan or some place."

It was as if he were announcing a winner in the bingo game.

"You ought to use your influence, Mrs. Latham. Old Swede's running around with that slant-eyed Mata Hari that Ben Farrell was married to. That babe is a smart operator . . . Corinne something or other, I forget——"

"Farrell, I expect, isn't it?"

Alice Cather's voice was as cool as a thin slice of cucumber in ice water.

"—Why don't you show Mrs. Latham the garden before it gets dark?" Alice Cather was going on pleasantly. "And I'm sure she's anxious to hear about your friends."

She'd moved a little, as I had, so we both had a direct view of Mary through half a dozen generals, one of whom was producing a package of bobby pins for a delighted woman in gray chiffon with a pair of diamond ear clips that would have bought a shipload of bobby pins in other times. Mary was still by her father, her arm in his, talking to a naval officer whose white starched coattail was flipped out like the wing of a crinoline kite. Her face was still radiant. She hadn't heard. I was sure of it, and so was her mother. There was a perceptible relaxation in the tiny crow's-feet at the ends of her eyelids. And it couldn't be plainer that she was determined to get the brash young man out of the room. I supposed in addition to everything she didn't want him to go on talking about slant-eyed Mata Hari's with the Japanese house man standing correct and politely unobtrusive less than three feet away.

She took him firmly by the arm. "You know the way, Captain."

I was sure then she didn't know his name either. That's the nice thing about the uniform; all you have to do is tell silver from gold, eagles from leaves and stars from both.

4

SHE LED THE TWO OF US TO A STAIRWAY OFF
the entrance hall. It wasn't quite dark yet outside, but
it was dusk and the grass was already silvered with
dew. We went down winding stone steps at the side
facing Ewa, as they say here—northeast as opposed to
Waikiki. Around the terrace above us, facing the mountains, mauka as opposed to makai, toward the sea, was
the lanai where Alice Cather had stood listening to
the redbird's evening call. The swimming pool was
cut out of the rock, and I could hear the water splash-
ing from it down into the ravine.

All I could think of, however, was Ben Farrell, and
Swede, and the half-caste girl that Ben had married
and that Swede Ellicott was going to marry now. I
wanted to ask the captain more about it, but I was afraid
to start him again and not be able to shut him off when
we got back to the house. And anyway he was not particularly sympathetic—in fact he was rather superior
and irritating.

"This must have cost plenty," he remarked. "I guess
Cather's family were missionaries. They're the ones

who cleaned up out here. You've heard about the Big Five?"

"The Cathers happened not to be," I said. I didn't know anything else about them, but Alice had told me that. "They were unsuccessful California Forty-niners and came on out here. And they aren't Big Five either."

We were going around the terrace toward the mountain side. It was unbelievably lovely, with the bank spilling showers of orchids growing out of moist tree fern wired to the rock.

"This is their air-raid shelter—it's a honey. Absolutely complete from soup to nuts."

He pointed at a low redwood door set in the bank. It looked much more like the entrance to an enchanted cavern in a fairy tale, with its ornamental iron hinges and lock and the fern growing around it on the mossy rocks, and pale-green and lemon-yellow orchids hanging over it. I'd started to say so, when behind us, out of the brooding silence of the twilight against the hills, came the single note followed by the long sliding see-saw of the redbird's call. It was so close and clear that remembering Alice Cather on the lanai I stopped and looked around, trying to locate it. And I stood, motionless at first and then rigid, just staring.

A man's face was there against the trees. It was nothing else, it was just a face . . . and it was not in the trees, it was against them. It stood out, plain and visible and perfectly motionless, as I stared, not really believing I was seeing it and yet unable to believe I wasn't.

In the curious visual quality of the dusk it was very white around the forehead under an indefinite hair-line, with cheeks that shaded into a dark stubble. I blinked my eyes quickly. It was still there, fixed and stationary in mid-air against the dense growth of green and dun-colored foliage. I couldn't see any eyes, but I had the feeling that they were there, fixed on me, piercing and unwavering. And it *was* there. I *could* see it.

"Look," I said. "Over there, in the trees."

The captain turned from the air-raid shelter door. I started to point, and had an instant queer feeling that it might be wiser not to.

"I don't see anything," he said.

I didn't either. There was nothing there. The face had gone. I was looking exactly where I'd been looking before. There was nothing there but the leaves.

"—I saw a face," I said. "A man's face."

He looked around at me. "A spy," he said gravely. Then he laughed. "Lady, don't start that around here . . . everybody'll just laugh at you. There's nothing here the Japs are interested in—they're too busy at home. Let's go get a drink."

I was still looking for the face, or for the formation of leaves and light and shade that had looked so extraordinarily like one. If it had been an hallucination it was a very vivid and solid one, and I knew it hadn't. It was a man's face. I had seen it, and the image in my mind was as sharply positive as if I saw it still. If it had been any one else with me, or if the face had had a torso and arms and legs, I'd have insisted on waiting. But I gave up too and moved reluctantly along.

There were more steps toward the house where it faced the mountains, and we went up them to the garden level. At the top I looked back. The face was there again, and this time I had no possible doubt about it. But it was there just an instant. It wasn't against the leaves this time so much as in them, and it blotted out sharply, as if a leafy branch had been drawn across it. It was still nothing but a face, chalky-white and stubbly-dark. In the half-light of the exotic twilight it made my flesh creep.

"What's the matter now, Mrs. Latham?"

"Nothing at all," I said pleasantly. I followed the captain across the lawn to the downstairs room where the bar was. At the end of the terrace I stopped again, but there was nothing back there, or nothing that I could see. And maybe, I thought for a moment, there hadn't been anything there at all, really; it could have been a trick of the light and my imagination. Or perhaps it was an Hawaiian custom for disembodied heads to float around against the trees. It was darker now, as if a curtain had been drawn down as the shafts of the dying sun made tangible plains of shadow slanting up to the top of the ridge, leaving it dark and sombre in the ravine.

Yet all the time I knew that the face in the woods was still there. I knew it was hidden in the shadowy trees, a face without a body, rigid and poised, watching.

It kept coming in and fading out of my mind, disturbing all the more because I found myself giving it eyes, in my mind, and a kind of stealthy intentness.—And then there came into my mind again the sight of those two white searching planes, flying very low, circling, that Swede Ellicott had pointed out from the window of the Moana lobby—and the short conversation that the major and I had had on the Pali. And once when I heard the redbird's call again, long after Stateside redbirds would have been asleep, I started so that my partner thought he'd trumped my trick. I looked over toward Alice, thinking again that it could have been the contagion of her panic on the lanai that was responsible. But she'd gone out of the room and they were settling accounts at her table.

When the guests left I stood for a moment on the lanai looking over the dark rim of wilderness down onto the myriad lights of the city by the sea. Pearl Harbor was a vast white glow off to the right, beyond it the darkness of spreading cane fields and the ragged outlines of mountains against the sky. Behind me, moving noiselessly around the room, the Japanese house man was folding the bridge tables and clearing up for the night. The two little maids in their blue kimonos had disappeared. I suppose it was because Pearl Harbor glowed so brilliantly, itself and as a symbol, that I unconsciously turned and watched the man, intent on his job inside.

He was short and stocky, with thick straight black

hair and a broad flat face, with nothing about him to indicate his age to me. I suppose I must at some point or other have read in the papers that a large percentage of the population of the Hawaiian Islands was Japanese, either alien or native born, but I hadn't really been prepared for the shock of seeing so many of them everywhere. It seemed to me I saw practically nothing else, but that was no doubt because I wasn't used to them and was so conscious of them as a people we were fighting a few thousand miles forward over the Pacific.

When a voice spoke beside me I started. Harry Cather and Mary had come back on the lanai from seeing their guests off. And what I was thinking must have been pretty evident in my face.

"Now, now, Grace," Harry said, laughing. "Don't start a spy hunt, will you? Servants are hard to get. I assure you Kumumato's all right. He's been around for years."

Mary Cather laughed too.

"You're all right, aren't you, Kumumato?" she called across the lanai.

He had probably heard his name anyway. He stopped with his tray of glasses, grinned broadly and nodded, and went on.

"It must be sort of tough, when they're loyal," Mary said, "being eyed by everybody. It's crazy, really. Kumumato's as much an American as we are. He was born here in Honolulu and he's got two sons in the A. J. Battalion in Italy. And he had a daughter killed on the 7th. You know the bombs the Japs dropped on the city didn't hit anything but Japanese property. Of course, people who don't know them and aren't used to them the way we are out here are always sort of shocked."

"Mainlanders don't quite see the picture," Harry Cather said. "It would be a little hard to put that many people in concentration camps, in the first place, and it would play hob with every kind of labor. Except in the defense plants. They're not allowed on military jobs. I don't say there aren't some black sheep. It wouldn't be human nature if there weren't a few, out of the hundred and fifty thousand right here on Oahu. But they're a practical people. Only forty families went back to their emperor, when they were all given the chance, at the beginning of the war. Not very many, was it?"

"No, it wasn't," I agreed. "Not out of a hundred and fifty thousand."

"And we're all pretty well tabbed here, by Internal Security. They've got us all fingerprinted and we carry civilian identification cards—every man, woman and child in the Islands. The curfew wasn't anything anybody took lightly—blackout at sundown, at first, and after the war moved out, off the streets at ten."

"I wish I'd been here all the time," Mary said. "Everything wouldn't have been so different if I'd seen it gradually. You can't imagine how different it looks now."

We'd moved along to the corner of the lanai where we could look down over the dark valley to the jewelled brilliance of the city, and up to the dark mountains, stretching in an endless chair against the sky.

"It's funny how an Islander feels strange when there's nothing but flat land and buildings everywhere," she said. "It smells different, here, and it feels different. Even if they have made a fortress out of it, it's still Oahu, and I love it. Did you know, Mrs. Latham, that in the early days in California the wealthy people used to send their children here to school? It was shorter than sending them across the plains or around the Horn. It seems odd, doesn't it, when you can get from here to Washington in thirty-six hours now. It's going to be a funny world, isn't it, when we're all under each other's feet and you can't get away from anybody very far."

She laughed suddenly.

"Remember how glad we were, Dad, when Aunt Norah moved just over to Maui, because it was eighty-eight miles away and it made her seasick to ride on boats? Now she can take a plane and be here in half an hour.—I hope she doesn't, as soon as she sees in the papers we're back home again."

"I believe we're safe," her father said, I thought rather dryly.

Mary laughed again. "Do you have relatives too, Mrs. Latham?"

"A few," I said.

"Well, it's wonderful to be back home, anyway," she went on. "Are you turning in, Dad?"

Harry Cather stopped a few steps off. "No, I'm going to get a book for Grace. *Hawaii, Off Shore Territory*, it's called. I think it's a very intelligent picture of the situation here."

Mary watched him until he disappeared around the angle of the living room . . . a little covertly, I thought at first. And in an instant I was sure of it.

She turned to me quickly when he'd gone.

"—Mrs. Latham," she said, lowering her voice almost to a whisper. "Do you mind if I ask you something? Did . . . did I hear the captain talking to you about . . . Swede Ellicott?"

My heart sank a little. If she'd heard that much I didn't see how she could have helped hearing the rest of it, including the fact that the old gang was there in Honolulu and the bit about the slant-eyed Mata Hari. I didn't know what to say to her, and I must have hesitated much longer than seemed natural under the circumstances, because she looked away.

"I'm sorry," she said. "I shouldn't have asked, should I? But I . . . I thought I heard his name. I wasn't sure. I seem to hear it a lot even when the room's empty and nobody could possibly be saying it."

She turned her head and gave me a quick smile.

"Crazy, isn't it? Maybe it's the atmosphere. The Hawaiians hear things—music, and drums. . . . They see things too. Maybe it's catching. I've seen Swede a dozen times since I got here—only it's always somebody else when I get up to him."

She stood there, her body resting lightly against the rail behind us, poking at the lau-hala mat with the silver toe of her slipper.

"I always thought I ought to explain to you what happened," she said quietly. "About me and Swede, I mean. You were so sweet to us both, it seemed a little . . . abrupt, just to have Mother call and say it was over, without . . . without anything else."

"It's not customary to go around explaining things like that," I said. I was curious nevertheless.

"I know. And there's really nothing to explain. It was just over, that's all. I guess it was too . . . well, too swell to last."

I looked around at her quickly. The note in her low velvety-throated voice was too warm and too wistfully tender not to be arresting, especially in view of Tommy Dawson's derisive "the little Cather." She was still looking down at the tip of her shoe poking the edge of the woven mat.

"I thought I was all over it," she said. "All the . . . the hurt part of it, anyway. But I guess I'm not. I thought getting home, away from running into his aunt all the time, and seeing places that reminded me of him, I'd get him out of my head. But it doesn't seem to work that way."

She looked around at me and smiled. "It doesn't make any sense, does it?"

Not to me it didn't, certainly. There was obviously

something very wrong somewhere. That might just possibly be the spot where the she-buzzard came in— but I didn't know. I still couldn't think of Alice Cather in such terms.

"Every time I think I see him it all comes back with a wallop, and of course I know it's because there are so many flyers around, and they do sort of look alike."

"Do you want to see him, Mary?" I asked.

She drew her breath quickly.

"Oh, no!" she said. "Oh, I couldn't bear it. I'd do something crazy that I'd regret the rest of my life. No, it's not that."

She stopped short then, looking at me oddly. "But of course, it is that, isn't it? I mean, I wouldn't always be thinking I see him if I didn't really want to, would I?"

"I guess not," I agreed.

She hesitated.

"I suppose I was just awful young," she said slowly. "I'd never been in love with anybody else before. It hit me too hard, I suppose. I just didn't stop to use my head. I can see it now, but it's a bit late, and it doesn't help very much. If I'd been . . . older, or been around more, I'd have known it was just an exciting game—for all four of them. I guess maybe I should have asked for a copy of the ground rules before I got so much involved."

She tried to laugh, but it wasn't very successful.

"And I'm not blaming them at all. Don't think that. It's myself I'm blaming. After all, I'd known Swede

only ten days, and that's not very long when you're
signing up for life, I suppose. So when he got away
and got to thinking it over he realized it didn't make
sense. And he couldn't very well write and tell me so,
I suppose. But I wish he had. It's just never hearing
at all that made it sort of . . . sort of tough."

She rested both hands behind her on the rail and bent
her body forward a little so that I couldn't see her
face.

"And it's not that so much either, really. I've tried
to figure it out. I certainly wouldn't have wanted him
to keep on with it when he didn't care about me any
more. I'd rather know beforehand than afterwards it
wasn't going to work out. That would be worse. That's
what made my Aunt Norah what she is, and she's grim.
It simply wrecked her pride—and that's what really
happened to me, I think, if I'd be honest about it."

She straightened up abruptly.

"Oh, dear, if I'd just taken it and shut up!" she
said quickly. "That's what makes it so painful. If I'd
only listened to Mother—but I didn't. I just didn't
believe it. I thought his letters were lost, or they'd
gone astray, or something, so I kept on writing. Even
when I *knew*. I couldn't believe it. I wrote one *awful*
job—I could die when I think of it! I poured the old
broken heart stuff all over the paper, reams of it. I
can't bear to look at myself in the mirror when I think
about it. I adored him, and he was wonderful, and I
worshipped him, and so on and so on. He must have

been bored sick, or maybe he thought it was funny. I don't know."

She turned her back to the soft glow from the living room and stood looking down over the black slope of the hills to the gleaming lights of the city.

"I keep telling myself it doesn't matter," she said quietly, after a moment. "That I should just chalk it up to experience, so it never happens again. But——"

"That's not very easy to do," I said, as gently as I could. "People have been telling themselves that since the beginning of time."

"I know. But that doesn't help any either. It's harder to get over anything when you've made it worse by being a terrible fool along with all the rest of it. If I'd written the letters I did and then burned them up, I wouldn't care so much. But I *sent* them. If I just hadn't been so . . . so *naked* about it—that's what makes it so . . . humiliating. And Mother's been *elegant*. She really has. Never a single 'Well, if you'd only listened to me, darling!' nor any business about 'You can't go on like this forever, dear.' Heaven knows there are plenty of men around here now, but she hasn't once tried to stick one of them down my throat or say how attractive any of them are. And *that's* self-control."

Her laugh was a sort of spontaneous bubbling-up that was gone as quickly as it came.

"Oh, well, it doesn't matter," she said softly. "It just doesn't matter. It doesn't matter at all, really."

5

THE SILENCE AND THE EERIE BROODING DARK-
ness stretching to black invisibility above and around
us down to the gay and garish brilliance of the million
lights of the city made it seem more poignant and
lonely and intense as she stood there, slim and lovely,
trying to teach her reluctant heart the wisdom that
hearts, for centuries, have been unwilling to learn.

I looked down at the white glow of the city again.
Swede Ellicott was down there somewhere . . . with
Corinne, no doubt. If Mary's pride as well as her heart
was hurt at this point, I wondered which would be hurt
the more if and when she knew. I hoped intensely just
then that she would never have to know at all. I hadn't
myself entirely got over the shock of learning Corinne
was Ben Farrell's widow. I could imagine without a
great deal of trouble the shock it would be to Mary
to find out that Swede was going to marry her next.
It was all completely beyond me. The naïvely romantic
notion I'd had at some point—it seemed a thousand light
years away just then—that it would be nice to bring
Mary and Swede together again gave me cold chills

up and down my spine when I thought of it. This was much too serious a business.

"—Here's Dad with your book," Mary said. "Let's go in. I wonder where Mother's got to?"

I'd been wondering about her mother too, only on a different level. In spite of what Mary had said about her, I still had what Tommy Dawson said, with conviction and no wavering ifs or buts, in the background of my mind. I wondered if what Mary thought was self-control was more than that. It might easily have been a sense of guilt, if, for instance, it had been her own fine Italian hand interfering with the due process of the United States mails. I wouldn't for an instant have put it past her. That's the trouble, perhaps, with perfect surfaces. They always conceal something, and it's very easy to suspect the worst.

She was in the entrance hall, actually, just coming up out of the stairway from the lower floor. I took Harry Cather's book and the three of us waited until Alice switched off the lights and closed the stairway door.

"I was just looking around, it's so lovely out there at night. I thought you were all going to bed. Good night."

She kissed her daughter lightly on the cheek.

"Kumumato'll turn out the lights, Harry. We're down this way, Grace. You must be exhausted. I'm going to give you a pill to make you sleep like an angel. The doctor gave them to me and they're wonderful. It takes a little time to get used to the climate out here."

That was puzzling, I thought, the climate being their basic claim to an earthly paradise out there. It was as puzzling as the quick barrage of words she was throwing out around us.

"Come along, Grace."

I said good night to Mary and Harry Cather and went with her.

"I'll get it for you now," she said.

She went into her room and came back with an orange capsule, and handed it to me before she turned on the light in my room across the passage from hers, at the end of the wing against the mountains. If either of us needed the sleeping pill it was her, I thought. In the brighter lights of the bedroom she looked drawn and curiously bloodless. Her eyes were drained and her cheeks drooped in two heavy lines along her nostrils. She looked nervously around the room.

"I think you'll find everything. It's cold up here at night. You've got a blanket. Good night, dear."

She started for the door, and stopped.

"Grace," she said. She hesitated for an instant. "Is it true Swede Ellicott is here, in Honolulu?"

"Yes, it is," I said.

She leaned her head against the door panel a moment and closed her eyes. Her cheeks were gray, and the lines drooped more heavily. She pressed her lips together to keep them from trembling.

"Swede Ellicott, Tommy Dawson and Dave Boyer,"
I said. "They're all here . . . all except Ben Farrell,
and he's dead."

"I know," she whispered. "I'm sorry."

She moved away from the door and came and sat
down on the side of the bed. She sat there a long time,
her eyes fixed sightlessly on the floor.

"Grace," she said then. "I want to see Swede. It
. . . it isn't true that he's interested in Corinne, is it?
It can't be. I don't believe it."

"It seems to be what they say," I said. "It probably
is true."

I was surprised at the way she spoke of her. "Do
you know her?"

"Yes. I know her. At least I know who she is. I
don't know her to speak to."

"Well, who is she?" I asked. I wanted to know.

She didn't answer at once. Then she said, "Oh, she's
just a girl in Honolulu, that's all. Not any Mata Hari
that I know of. It's hardly sporting to call her that.
I think she's just one of a great many young women
here who'd like to marry an American boy—being of
mixed ancestry herself."

She lapsed into silence again.

"I was very foolish," she said abruptly after a moment. "I should have let Mary marry Swede, I suppose. I wonder. . . . Perhaps if I talked to Tommy,
or Dave . . ."

She got up and started over to the lanai to get out

of the light and away a little. I suppose I was looking at her without a great deal of sympathy. I was feeling pretty grim about her, as a matter of fact. I also knew it wasn't going to help matters for her to talk to Tommy or Dave Boyer.

She stopped short on the threshold.

"I'm going to draw your blind down, dear. It really gets cold up here at night."

It looked like an afterthought, or something, to me, as I watched her roll down the heavy woven matting until it covered the opening onto the lanai.

"That's better," she said. "The light won't annoy you in the morning."

She tied the cord down to the hook in the wood door frame. I watched her with a vague uneasiness.

She came back to the foot of the bed and stood there uncertainly. "Oh, it's no use, I guess," she said. Then she turned abruptly and looked directly at me for the first time. I was appalled at the sudden passion ravaging her face, blazing in her eyes.

"I've got to get Mary away from here, Grace! I've got to! I can't just sit and watch her life being ruined this way—it's too horrible! I thought if she and Swede . . . oh, but it's no use. Not now. Not if Corinne has stepped in. That would be ghastly for her—simply ghastly. And I won't have her hurt *that* way. That's more than I can stand. Oh, Grace, it's such a mess! I wish I were dead, I wish none of us had ever been born!"

I've seen people have hysterics and wish they were dead, but Alice Cather wasn't hysterical in any possible sense of the word. She was trembling with passion, but she was dry-eyed and controlled, with none of the ashen-gray terror she'd shown earlier, hearing the red-bird's call from across the ravine. She stood for a moment and then went slowly across to the door.

"I'm afraid I'm being rather difficult this evening," she said. "I'm still tired, I guess. And it was such a shock to find out about Ben, and to find Swede here after I thought we'd seen the last of him. I guess I weakened for a moment.—But only a moment," she added. She managed to smile. "Don't say anything to Mary, please. I don't want her to know. Maybe they'll be sent somewhere else. I know a good many of the officers at Hickam."

She put her hand on the door knob.

"Do take that pill and get some rest—and be sure to keep the blind drawn. I haven't had the pool cleaned out, and there may be mosquitoes. There's malaria, you know, and dengue fever."

I knew there wasn't, but I knew before that that she wasn't telling the truth. She'd had some other shock. The reaction from hearing about Ben Farrell and Swede couldn't have been that long delayed. It was something else. I wondered. There's no malaria in the Island of Oahu. Mosquitoes live in lowland marshes, not in mountain swimming pools. And that was not all. It came to me with a chilling uneasiness that made me look skeptically at the orange capsule in my hand and take it to the bathroom and put it quietly down the drain. Redbirds don't call in the middle of the night and faces don't move in trees without bodies to go with them . . . not in Oahu or anywhere else. Or if they did, I decided I didn't want to be so sound asleep I wouldn't know it.

It took me a long time to get to sleep without the capsule, however. My mind was like a blindfolded beast of burden, going around an interminable tread-mill of confusion and bewildering cross-currents, and the face in the trees kept creeping closer and closer until I thought I was seeing it in every shifting shadow in the room. But I must have gone to sleep finally, because suddenly with a horrible abruptness I was awake, sharply and instantly, stiff with apprehension and absolutely frigid, my heart an aching motionless weight inside me.

There was some one in my room. Where the woven lau-hala mat was that Alice Cather had drawn down was an open luminous space. Framed in it was a tall figure, groping to fasten the cord to hold it up that Alice Cather had tied to hold it down.

I lay on my side, my eyes open, staring, terrified, my throat constricted in a tortured knot.

The figure moved suddenly, silent and lithe as a great cat, flattening itself against the wooden frame of the opening, motionless then as a part of it. Some one else was on the lanai. I could hear a soft swish of steps on the matting. I saw the man's hand move toward his hip and rest there and move forward again. The long naked blade of a knife glinted in his hand. If I could have screamed then I would have, but I was sick and paralyzed with fear and no sound would come. Yet I knew I had to, had to warn whoever was coming . . . and then the cry I was forcing from my throat died before I ever uttered it.

"—Roy! Oh, God, not that room! Here—come quickly!"

It was Alice Cather. In the faint glow of the light from her room around the lanai I could see her. And she knew him, was calling him by name.

The man flashed forward onto the lanai. He was tall and very thin. His forehead was white and he was unshaven. His head was covered with leaves, his suit pale and spotted, like the camouflage suits the marines wear in the jungle . . . and I knew then, as he moved away, like something out of the jungle, swiftly and without effort or sound, why I had seen only the face against the trees.

Then the lanai was empty. The cold air from the mountains swept through the door and rustled over the straw mats on the floor. I didn't dare, at first, to move or more than breathe. And as I did, silently and more painfully than I can say, there was some one else on the lanai. The soft slipping tread of footsteps came like a horrible whisper to my tense sharpened hearing, coming closer and closer, until they were there at my door. A white coat glistened for an instant in the dim suffused glow of light, and a silver tray glistened. It was the Japanese house servant Kumumato, taking food to the man who had crept silently, like an animal, out of the wilderness in the night.

6

"OH, MY DEAR, I'M SORRY—DID I WAKE YOU?"
Alice Cather came in from the hall. And she did
wake me. I hadn't been asleep more than a couple of
hours, however, and seeing her there, amazingly fresh
in a white piqué dress, her hair damp around the edges
from a dip in the pool, I blinked my eyes and thought
perhaps it was all a nightmare. In the brilliant clarity
of the early morning it was hard to believe it really
had happened. Dreams can have such intense reality.
But I knew it wasn't a dream as soon as I sat up in bed.
Alice Cather had crossed the room too quickly. She
bent over at the threshold of the lanai, picked something up off the floor and thrust it into the pocket of
her skirt. I saw before she did it that it was a short
strand of cord, and I looked quickly up at the curtain
rolled unevenly and fastened to the top of the door
frame. Where the loop in the cord had been were two
clean-cut ends. It wasn't a dream, and in particular the
murderous-looking steel blade I'd seen wasn't a dream
either.

"Did our prowler disturb you last night?" she said.

"Prowler?"

My surprise at the word was so genuine that she misunderstood it. Her relief was very definite. She moved over to the dressing table and went through an elaborately casual business of pressing the wave deeper into her hair. In the mirror I saw she wasn't as fresh-looking as I'd thought, first waking. She should have taken the advice she'd given me about rouge.

"Yes, we had a prowler." She smiled at me. "They have a jungle training school the other side of the Island. Whether the man really got lost, which is possible, of course, or was AWOL I don't know. He got up here on the lanai, but I was awake. I must say he was more frightened than I was, poor lad. I woke Kumumato and we fed him and put him out on the Pali road. I hope he got back all right. He was homesick more than anything else, I think. He's been out here thirty-three months. Can you imagine that?"

She got up and went over to the lanai. She'd explained the man in the jungle suit—except for the knife, and except for her frantic half-stifled *"Roy! My God, not that room!"*—and Kumumato's tray, but she hadn't explained why the curtain with the loop cut clean from the cord was rolled up instead of down the way she'd left it. And I had a feeling that she was working on that one now.

"I hope I didn't disturb you when I pulled up the curtain?" she asked.

"No, you didn't," I said. It was perfectly true, if

truth mattered at a point when the knife could have cut my throat as easily and silently as it cut the curtain cord.

"It was so close," she said. "I thought we were getting Kona weather. They call it a sick wind, when it comes from the south. But it seems to have cleared."

She went out on the lanai and straightened a cushion in a long bamboo chair.

"We usually breakfast just along outside the dining room, if you'd care to slip on something and join us. And listen, my dear—please don't mention my prowler, will you? Harry's so upright he'd be furious at me for not reporting the man to Colonel Saffron. I only mentioned it in case you woke up and were alarmed at all."

"I won't say a word," I said. "And I'll take a shower and be with you in a minute."

When I got out there were floating veils of mist over the mountain clefts. Across the ravine a heavy rain was falling, but the Cathers' terraced lawns and gardens were a pool of brilliant sunshine. As I came to the corner of the lanai where we'd stood last night, looking down on Honolulu and the sea and up to the dark ridges of the hills, I heard Alice's voice.

"—Insist, won't you, Harry . . . really! I mean, I *want* her to stay here."

The three of them were there around a low breakfast table. Alice put down the silver coffee pot and smiled around at me.

"We're plotting against you, Grace darling. We're not going to let you go back down to Waikiki. You've got to stay here with us. You'll be so much more comfortable."

Prepared as I was, I still found it difficult to believe. I should have thought the one thing Alice Cather would want, as much as I wanted myself, was for me to get out and go down to Waikiki as fast as possible. I couldn't imagine for the life of me why she'd want me to stay.

"We'd be very pleased, indeed, if you would stay," Harry Cather said. It was hardly insistent, but it was certainly very cordial.

"It's much better up here, Mrs. Latham," Mary said. She was slathering half a Washington week's ration of butter on a small golden corn muffin. "I can drive you any place you want to go. I don't start my job with the Red Cross for a couple of weeks."

I shook my head.

"Thanks, a lot," I said. "But I've got to get back."

I was thinking about the man in my room, and the long gleaming knife. No fantastic tale Alice Cather could tell me made that any the less grim, remembering it. He might be gone for the moment, but I had no way of knowing whether he was gone for good or not.

"No, darling—you've *got* to stay."

Harry Cather smiled and picked up his paper. "You might as well, Grace. When Alice makes up her mind . . ."

He was interrupted by an abrupt bang and clatter from the inside of the house and a woman's voice, high-pitched and decisive.

"—Have they started leaving the house *empty* now?" it demanded. "Harry! Where are you?"

The effect on the breakfast table on the lanai was extraordinary. Mary Cather's spoon of orange-colored papaya stopped just in front of her open mouth, which stayed open. Alice's coffee cup halted in mid-air, and the paper Harry Cather was opening remained stationary, for seconds. Then he closed it and laid it quietly down on the floor beside his chair, the expression on his face indescribable. I don't think I've ever been conscious of three people's hearts sinking so in unison. It wasn't just dismay. It was a kind of hopelessness, nearly despair, that Alice Cather was the first to articulate.

"Oh, *no*, Harry!"

She put her coffee cup down, bent her head forward in her hand and closed her eyes.

"Oh, *Dad!*" Mary looked across at her father. "*Please!*"

Harry drew a deep breath, pushed back his chair and got up.

"Just keep quiet, both of you. Don't say anything at all."

He raised his voice. "We're here, Norah!"

As he started over to the door he turned back to me. "It's my sister, Grace. She can be difficult at times."

I think I could have told both, seeing the woman coming through the dining room. She was tall and spare and rigid as a spinster in a primitive painting. She had her brother's large dark eyes and high forehead but none of the mild kindliness that made him seem less gaunt and austere. Her hair was gray, her skin brown and weather-beaten and she had on a purple and white print dress that had seen far, far better days.

"I hardly expect a welcome or what have you and what have you," she said. There was a sharp overtone of martyrdom in her voice. "I always have to remind myself that I have a *right* in——"

"We have a guest, Norah, if you don't mind." He stood aside as she came on out. "Mrs. Latham, my sister Mrs. Bronson."

Mrs. Bronson dismissed me with a curt nod.

"So you've come back, Alice, now it's safe and there's no rationing over here to worry about."

She turned to her niece. "Well, Mary. You've certainly improved, in looks anyway. I thought you were going to get married. I thought that was what your mother took you to Washington for. What happened? You were engaged, weren't you?"

Mary had got to her feet, as awkward as an adolescent, and stood with her cheeks crimson. "I'm sorry, Aunt Norah. I was engaged, but I'm not now."

Mrs. Bronson dismissed that. "Well.—I'll have Kumumato unpack my bags. I'm spending the night."

Alice Cather looked sharply at her husband, her face tense and quite pale.

"I'm sorry, Norah." Harry Cather's voice was polite but very firm. "We've asked you to let us know when you're coming over. It happens the guest room is occupied. Mrs. Latham here is staying with us. You'll have to go to the hotel."

"My dear Harry," his sister said sharply, "I assure you I'd prefer a hotel to staying where I'm not wanted. But there are no rooms. I phoned over——"

"I'll get you one, Norah—right now."

He strode into the house. His sister hesitated for a moment, and then, ignoring the three of us, began examining things with an air that must have been maddening.

"I see you've put in a new rail and what have you."

"Termites," Alice said.

"We never used to have termites, and repairs are expensive."

Mother and daughter exchanged a quick glance. Two bright red spots burned in Mary's cheeks, her eyes were hot and bright. Alice shook her head slightly.

"If you have no objection, Alice, I'll look around——"

If I've ever seen living fear leap into anybody's face it was in Alice Cather's then. She was out of her chair in a flash.

"I object *intensely*."

Mrs. Bronson stopped short, staring at her.

"You looked it over less than a month ago. Nothing's been done or changed since."

Alice Cather's words came out as if she were biting them off in white-hot chunks.

"We're not going through that again. We're not going to have another bill of complaints about the air-raid shelter—Harry paid for that out of his own pocket three years ago. The house may be part yours but it's also part Harry's, and he has a right to live here in peace. He doesn't come and pry around yours because it's part his, and you're not going to pry around here."

Harry Cather, back on the lanai, looked a little startled, I thought, at her sudden vehemence.

"—I have a room for you, Norah," he said. "Kumumato's put your bags in the car. He'll take you down."

Mrs. Bronson, I saw, was not a woman easily put out. "I'm seeing the house before I go, Harry."

"That's your privilege," Harry Cather said shortly.

Alice was on her feet again, her face white. "Norah is not going around the house this morning, Harry," she said. "The beds aren't made. The kitchen isn't in order. She can look it over tomorrow or the next day, but not this morning. Either this house is mine or it's hers. If she goes around now, Harry, I'm leaving, and I'm not coming back. I mean what I'm saying. I've had all of this I'm going to take."

—*He is still in the house,* I thought. *He is still in the house. The man in the jungle suit is still in the house. The man named Roy is still in the house.* It was going around and around in my head like a crazy jingle they'd sing in a kindergarten, over and over again. He was there, and Alice Cather was terrified for fear her husband and her sister would find him. Well, it was her business, I thought, not mine. I looked surreptitiously at my watch, very glad I was leaving. Nothing could have persuaded me to stay.

Harry Cather stood looking blankly at his wife.

"—I'm simply fed up, Harry."

"All right, if that's the way you feel."

He turned to his sister. "You'll have to come to-morrow, Norah. Alice is still tired from her trip."

If only men didn't always bring that one out, I thought. Norah Bronson's dark eyes appraised her sister-in-law for a long moment with a singular lack of sympathy.

"I'll be here tomorrow," she said.

Alice stood holding the back of the bamboo chair in front of her until the two of them had disappeared through the house. She moved then, not too steadily, and sat down. She rested her head on the back of the chair and closed her eyes.

"Oh, that will! That stupid, stupid will!"

She moved her head slowly from side to side.

"—'That my three children may live in peace and amity, each with the others.' And all they've ever done is quarrel, quarrel, quarrel. It's wicked."

We were silent for a moment.

"Well," Mary said practically, "she's gone, now. Maybe she won't come back. I wonder what on earth brought her so early in the——"

For the third time Alice Cather started up from her chair. The color was draining out of her face. She took a quick step forward, hitting the side of the table. The dishes rattled sharply and a water goblet tipped over.

"Norah!" she cried. "Norah!"

She ran around the table into the house.

Mary Cather looked at me wide-eyed.

"For Heaven's sake," she said. She picked up the goblet and put a napkin down to sop up the water. "Everybody's gone nuts, completely nuts. There must be a Kona wind."

She wrung the water out of the napkin and put it flat over the rail to dry.

"What a family," she said dismally. "That's the trouble about the will. It left everything jointly to all three of them, Dad and Aunt Norah and Uncle Roy. Only we never mention Uncle Roy. He's Kapu. He disgraced the family—married a Japanese house servant, I think it was. I don't know all of it. He lives in Java, or somewhere out there. Mother was in love with him, once, they——"

She broke off abruptly and looked at me with a sudden bewildered uneasiness.

"What's the matter? You . . . you don't know my Uncle Roy, do you—by any chance?"

She was staring at me, quite pale, and I suppose I'd been staring, blank-faced and open-mouthed, at her ever since she first spoke his name, only she'd been too pre-occupied pressing the wrinkles out of the sodden napkin to notice. The name alone would have been enough, Heaven knew, with her mother's frantic exclamation still in my ears from the night before. The rest of it was a piling up, coming so casually and innocently, and without any awareness of what it meant in terms of a situation right under the roof with us, that I was appalled.

If her Uncle Roy lived in Java, just for one thing, he was to say the least an amazing distance from home. Her mother's being in love with him once was as amazing, in a different way. It explained why she'd taken him in out of the jungle, and why, if he needed to be taken in in the middle of the night, he would appeal to her rather than to his own brother. It also explained, I supposed, why his portrait hung over the mantel in her sitting room. But it left even more, one way and another, that it did not explain, and in fact only confused a terrific lot.

"—*Do* you know him?"

Her eyes were wide and her face still quite pale.

"Oh, no," I said quickly, "Of course not. I've never been in Java. I was thinking about something else— something I've forgotten to do. It just struck me."

"Oh," she said. She drew a deep breath of relief. "I just wondered. I . . . I'm awfully curious about him myself. He was . . . oh, lots of things—a famous swimmer for one, almost as famous as Duke Kahana-moku. I was going to warn you too, if you did happen to, for Heaven's sake to keep quiet about him. Just his name makes Dad livid and gets Mother fearfully upset. They used to be scared to death he'd show up, but the war fixed that. He . . . he's supposed to be dead, but that's just a manner of speaking. They don't know I know it."

She smiled. "It's funny how parents expect children to be bright in school and blind, deaf and dumb around the house, isn't it?"

She looked away across the sunlit tree tops to the sparkling sea.

"Of course, Aunt Norah's right about Washington. I might as well tell you all of it. The reason Mother objected to Swede was he didn't have any money. You see, according to this will she was talking about everything goes into a foundation. All I get if Dad should die is what he made himself, which isn't much if anything. I'd have to go to work, and Mother can't see that. She doesn't see things that way. She has some funny ideas. But that's because she's had a rotten deal in lots of ways," she added quickly. "She was a governess when Dad married her. I guess that can be pretty bad."

The color deepened in her cheeks. She took the napkin off the rail and folded it up with concentrated attention.

"Look, Mrs. Latham," she said. "Last night, after I went to bed I got the idea that you might have thought maybe Mother had something to do with . . . with my not hearing from Swede. But that isn't true."

She laughed with a sudden quite spontaneous gaiety.

"She can be an awful Jesuit . . . the ends justifying the means sort of thing. But we'd figured on that. Swede's aunt—the one that lives next door to you—she was our post office. We thought of asking you first, but we didn't quite dare so we asked her. If he'd written I'd have got the letters."

She looked at me and smiled.

"Well, that's that," she said. "I just wanted to have the record straight. Now I'll shut up. Have some coffee, will you, Mrs. Latham?"

Her father and mother were coming along the lanai from the wing at the other end of the house as she handed me a cup.

"Did you catch her, Mama dear?"

Alice Cather shook her head silently.

Harry looked at me with a slightly rueful and I thought somewhat apologetic smile. "I'm afraid you're stuck, Grace," he said. "You're going to have to stay with us. I got my sister your room. There simply weren't any others. You don't really mind, do you . . . ?"

7

A THURBER DRAWING OF A QUANDARY WOULD, I think, have been a very fair portrait of me as I got myself dressed to go down to Waikiki to get my things so Aunt Norah could have my room at the crowded hotel. Uppermost in my bewildered mind, and most completely inexplicable, was Uncle Roy. The simplest explanation of him, on the face of it, I thought, seemed to be that he had escaped from somewhere. People didn't hide out in the mountains and creep in like a thief in the night. It was equally obvious that however famous a swimmer he might have been, he hadn't swum from Java to Oahu, Territory of Hawaii. It was too far. Java could, however, have been what they wanted Mary to believe if he was in prison, say, for something horrible . . . or in an asylum. That made more sense than Java. It also made the long knife he carried a little more frightening.

I suddenly thought of Alice Cather's first intimation that he was there, when she heard the redbird's call on the lanai outside her sitting room—a signal, obviously, that she must have known very well. The terror she was in then did not seem to indicate she was very much in love with the signaller. Unless . . . I dismissed that quickly. Her emotions were clearly no problem of mine. My problem was more personal and immediate, and it was, quite simply, how I was going to stay there without getting my throat cut.

And more puzzling than Harry Cather's brother was why she wanted me to stay.

I picked up my bag and stopped abruptly. One thing suddenly popped into my mind: the reason for her extraordinary *volte face* when she knocked over the water goblet, and why Aunt Norah was there and insisting on going over the house. Norah Bronson knew, some way, that the other brother was there, and Alice was aware that she knew . . . just too late.

I was wondering about that when Alice appeared at my door.

"Ready, darling? I'm going with you. I've got to stop at the Red Cross."

Mary was waiting with the car in the drive outside.

"I want to stop a moment at the cottage," Alice said as we got in.

Coming in in the later afternoon, wind-blown from the Pali, I hadn't realized the Cathers' place was as extensive as it was. A wide band of trees and shrubs, almost tropical in density, hid the house from the road. Off to our left was a small cottage that I'd noticed vaguely and assumed was the gardener's or a porter's lodge. It had hibiscus, scarlet and yellow and pink, around it, and the same sloping roof and overhanging eaves that the main house had. I could see now it was closed and unoccupied.

Mary drew up at the end of a path off the drive.

"I'll be just a minute," her mother said.

We watched her go up the path, Mary smiling a little.

"I wonder what she's got in her busy little mind now," she said. "That was my Uncle Roy's cottage. He built it when he and Dad had a terrific row just after their father died and left the three of them here to live in the big house together. Oh, dear, what a family. That was before he went to live in Java. My father went out after him, and that's where he met Mother."

She looked at me grave-eyed.

"Do families always have to fight?"

"They fight over estates," I said, "and who gets what, more than anything else, I expect. Or so lawyers tell me."

"And they say civil war is the worst kind. Boy, are they right.—What's the matter?"

I said, "Nothing." I was thinking of the cottage and Roy Cather going to live in it, before he went to Java, and wondering. But it wasn't, obviously, where he was now. Alice was throwing open the doors and shutters and putting up the windows around the lanai.

"Did you ever notice," Mary asked, "that you can always tell when Mother's plotting something? Just watch her. I'll bet she's figuring something right now so Aunt Norah won't be able to move up to the cottage. I'll bet anything we have guests before supper . . . Waves or Wacs or a bunch of tired submariners from the Royal Hawaiian.—What Mother wants, she gets."

She laughed and switched on the motor. "Let's pretend we're dreadfully surprised."

I may say we didn't have to pretend. And surprise isn't quite the word. Consternation fits what happened better. But that was later, and consternation is only the shadow of a word that would fit what happened in between.

We left Alice at the ramshackle painted wooden barracks that houses the Pacific Ocean area headquarters of the Red Cross, behind St. Andrew's Cathedral, and went out to Waikiki. It never occurred to me, as Mary let me out in front of the hotel and took the car along to park it, that the simple business of coming to get my bags would be in any way catastrophic. The only person it even entered my mind we might meet that I'd prefer to avoid was Aunt Norah. And I wasn't even thinking about Aunt Norah then . . . I was thinking about going back to the house where Uncle Roy was the unseen guest, and wishing there was some decent way to avoid it without having to sleep in a foxhole on the beach at Waikiki.

I got my key at the desk and came back toward the door. The lobby was already crowded with officers coming and going. I stood waiting for Mary out of the

main line of traffic to the elevators, without any intimation of disaster of any conceivable kind. Then my heart
sank with a sickening jolt. Not three feet away from me
was Swede Ellicott, and with him was the half-caste girl
Corinne. She was dressed in white again, her shiny black
hair in a high smooth pompadour off her broad forehead,
her brown eyes laughing, one hand tucked in Swede's
arm, with an air of possessive intimacy that wasn't possible to mistake.

Outside across the street I could see Mary just getting out of the car where she'd parked it. She was
locking the door. In another minute or two she'd be
across the street and up the steps into the lobby. And
Swede saw me as quickly as I saw him, too late for me
to slip behind a pair of naval officers next to me and
disappear.

"Hello, there, Grace," he said.

I suppose the consternation I felt for an awful instant must have been more than visible in my face,
because his went very sober, abruptly.

"Hello, Swede," I said.

I think he would have skipped everything from there
on if the girl hadn't looked over at me and back up
at him, so that he couldn't very well not introduce us
without being rude to her. And anyway, I was making
one of the noblest efforts to smile that I think I've ever
been called on to make.

"—I'd like you to meet Corinne Farrell. Mrs.
Latham, Corinne. You remember Ben, Grace."

"Yes, indeed," I said. I put out my hand automatically. Corinne's was very small and soft, like a kitten's, and warm as it touched mine a moment.

"How do you do," she said. "Ben used to talk about you, and Swede told me you were here."

Her accent was not foreign, certainly, but it had a strange quality that made it different from most Americans' and yet hard for me to place. It was precise and her voice rather high-pitched.

And Mary was starting across the street.

"I was sorry to hear about Ben," I said.

"Oh, yes, it was very sad."

I don't know why I didn't have the feeling that there was any profound regret either in her voice or the way the laughter went out of her face for an instant to come back again almost as quickly. It didn't dim the radiant possessiveness of her smile as she looked back up at Swede. His face was still sober and his brows contracted a little, but again I didn't have the impression that that was as much for Ben as it was irritation with me for my surprise and dismay seeing him and the girl together. I could see he was putting it down to racial snobbishness on my part.

I glanced at the door again. I was really sick. It seemed so ghastly, someway, for Mary to have to meet him like this. It was fate, maybe, but it was a blind and very cruel fate. And if there was ever an answer to an unspoken prayer, it came then . . . in the form of a long line of khaki-colored trucks filled with GI's in fatigue clothes. Mary was still on the curb on the other side of the street. I could tell that by the way the GI's were craning their necks and waving as the trucks lumbered by.

"We're just going to have lunch, Mrs. Latham," Corinne said, smiling at me. I thought her eyes, quicker and sharper and more on the alert than Swede's, had followed mine out the door and that there was a curious appraising flicker in them as they turned to me. "Why don't you join us? I think Swede has much to talk to you about. I think so."

"Sure, Grace . . . come on."

The trucks had passed and I saw Mary run across the street, the sunlight glistening on her hair as she reached the sidewalk. The meeting, staved off a moment, was inevitable now, and my heart went down quietly and stayed in the pit of my stomach.

"I'm awfully sorry," I said. "I'd love to, but I've got an engagement—I'm waiting for a friend."

That was when I knew Corinne had seen Mary Cather too. Her face did not change exactly, or outwardly anyway, but it was as if somebody had quietly tilted the slats in a Venetian blind, shuttering out the direct rays of light from the room of her mind. Her hand tightened a little on Swede's arm as she turned him toward the dining room. Then my heart rose again. Mary, already on the bottom step, turned and stopped as some one called her, and held out her hand, laughing. Corinne saw that too.

"Another time, I hope, Mrs. Latham," she said. "Come along, Swede. We're keeping Mrs. Latham, and we won't get a table if we don't hurry."

Swede nodded. "Good-bye, Grace." I thought he was still a little troubled as he moved away with her. And it was just in a fraction of the nick of time. Mary came running into the lobby.

"I'm sorry," she said breathlessly. "First there was a line of trucks and then a friend of Dad's. What on earth's the matter? You didn't run into Aunt Norah, did you?"

"No," I said. "Come along—here's an elevator."

She started over with me. I could see Corinne, standing alone, looking across at us. There was no smile on her red lips and no laughter in her eyes. Swede, his back to us, was over at the telephone by the room desk.

"Oh, look!" Mary touched my elbow. "See that girl? Her name's Corinne, and she's a wonderful dancer. Her hula's lovely."

I didn't somehow want to look at Corinne again.

"Are you coming, darling," I said, "or aren't you?"

Having so narrowly escaped this far I couldn't bear to give up. I gave her a little push into the waiting elevator . . . and Swede Ellicott turned, caught my eye and nodded at me just as the door of the elevator closed.

"You're just like Mother," Mary said. "Every time I used to want to go to see Corinne dance she hit the ceiling, and really she's lovely. A real hula is beautiful."

I didn't say anything. It's hard to explain the relief
I felt as we got out on my floor and went along the
corridor to my former room. In any one of half a
dozen fractions of a moment there in the lobby the
laughing violet-eyed girl with me now could have
changed into one I hoped I'd never have to see. And
I could still see in my mind the shuttered unsmiling
mask that Corinne Farrell turned on us as we started
for the elevator. There was no doubt, I thought, that
she knew a great deal more about Mary Cather than
Mary knew about her. I thought there was no doubt
either that she had it in her mind to keep Swede Ellicott, by fair means or any others, and also that Mary
would be tragically unprepared for a kind of attack
that Corinne would be an old and no doubt established
hand at. It was better for her that none of their paths,
hers and Swede's or hers and Corinne's and Swede's,
should ever cross. It was sheer chance that they almost
had just then, and even sheerer chance that they had
not.

We got my things, quickly. We got out of the hotel
while they were still in the dining room—and without
running into Aunt Norah—and went to the Outrigger
Club for lunch. It was half-past four when we drove
up Nuuanu Avenue. It was brilliant and clear until
we came to the Pali road, and then it was raining cats
and dogs. We turned left through the lichen-covered
gates of the Cathers' place under the mountains, and
it was all brilliant and clear again. The cottage furniture

was all out on the lanai, and Kumumato and the two little maids were working like beavers, scrubbing and dusting and airing.

Mary stopped the car. "I'll go see what's happening," she said.

She ran up the path to the little house. I saw her talking to Kumumato, and in a moment she was back.

"Do you mind walking in the rest of the way?" she asked. "They've got an awful lot of old stuff Mother wants moved out, and she isn't home yet. I thought I'd leave the car for them. Kumumato can bring your bags when he comes."

"Surely," I said.

"Let's cut down and go this way and I'll show you my room. I'm in the other wing. There are a lot of orchids down there."

We went off the road down to the left through a wooded gully, though I don't know if gully is the right word for a place where the orchids grew in pale gorgeous showers under the trees.

"Be careful, it's wet," she said.

It was not only wet, it was muddy, and our shoes were caked. It must have been raining worse than cats and dogs there recently.

"Let's go back—we can't make it," Mary said. We scrambled up another path that was muddy too and that took us out a little to the left of the main entrance. Our shoes were a mess.

"Just take them off," Mary said, slipping out of

hers and parking them at the door. "The Japanese have a lot of very sensible customs. Kumumato'll get them. We'll go for a swim. I'll get my suit and bring you one till your things get in. I won't be but a second."

She skipped barefooted off toward her wing, and I, feeling a little awkward walking around anybody else's house in my stocking feet, went out onto the lanai to go to mine.

I put my bag on the bed and started over to close the door leading to the inside hall. I wasn't, for some reason, even thinking about Uncle Roy. The busy rushing about down in town where there were people and shops would have wiped him out of my mind for the time being even if it hadn't been for that scene in the lobby of the Moana, and if I was thinking about anything it was whether Mary would remember to bring me a cap so my hair wouldn't get wet. I suppose that knowing Alice Cather wasn't at home and Kumumato was up at the cottage may have put me off guard too. Anyway, I started over to the door to close it, and I stopped quicker than I ever remember stopping before. Alice Cather's door was partly open, and I could hear a man's voice as plainly as if he were in my room.

"—a bargain," I heard. "Not as good a bargain as I hoped to make, Alice. But a bargain."

It was a voice such as I'd never heard before, quiet and arrogant and dark, and with some entirely indescribable quality that made me shiver suddenly, standing there. I'd thought, at first, that he was talking on the phone, and I glanced quickly around at the lanai to make sure it was as close, and as accessible, as I'd thought it was. It was Alice Cather's voice there that stopped me a second time.

"I'm only keeping my end if you keep yours, Roy."

"Of course, my dear."

"And let me tell you, Roy. I'm not being funny. You can stay here till you can get away—as long as you do stay. I don't know why you're here, and I don't trust you, and I don't believe anything you say——"

"Oh, come, Alice . . . don't be heroic."

It was playful and mocking, the man's voice, and in some way still more frightening. Then it changed sharply.

"When are you going to get her out of here?"

"I've told you I *can't*, Roy! Harry asked her. She was nice to us in Washington. She'd think it was very funny if I asked her to leave. I don't dare!"

I swallowed down the cold lump that had risen in my throat and stood there, motionless, any sense of ethics I may have had about eavesdropping gone in a flash. If I was being used, it was clearly my business to find out what for and why.

"She won't bother you if you stay where you're put and quit prowling around the house. She didn't hear you last night. I got the cord you cut before she saw it this morning."

The man laughed a little, almost noiselessly. "I think she heard me, Alice. I think so."

My feet were like lumps of ice-cold lead and my spine crawled. I don't know how to describe the menace in that quiet voice.

"I have trained ears, Alice. I think she woke. She stopped breathing——"

"No, Roy! You're being crazy!"

Alice Cather's voice had a sudden frantic note in it.

"She took a sleeping pill I gave her. I asked her this morning. She drew a complete blank."

"You're not lying to me, Alice?"

The menace in the slow dark voice was terrifying.

"I wouldn't like you to lie to me, my dear."

"Stop it, Roy. I'm telling you the truth."

"Then why is she here? Who is this colonel? Where is he?"

That was sharp and staccato. I drew my breath quickly and held it for a moment, understanding nothing at all.

"His name is Primrose and he's a special agent.—Let go of me, Roy, I'm trying to tell you! Military intelligence, something—nobody knows. I tell you he's been watching me. He was in San Francisco when I got there, and so was she. He was in Washington, New York, Charleston, everywhere, since the broadcast. I don't know how they traced it. He was everywhere. I know he's coming here, if he isn't here already. That's why she's here. She's watching me for him. I know it. That's why she came out when we did. She doesn't know what she's doing. She's supposed to be observing rest camps and USO's, but that's absurd. She's not bright enough to work on her own, but he uses her. That's what he's doing now. As long as she's here it's all right."

There was silence for an instant. I heard her catch her breath in a panic-stricken sob.

"—I'm telling you the truth, Roy."

"You're not lying, trying to keep me in that hole?" the dark voice said. "Not lying about her connections . . . to save yourself, Alice?"

8

I WAS WONDERING VERY MUCH MYSELF, JUST
then. It was indescribably strange, hearing myself and
Colonel John Primrose made into a joint team trailing
her—for what reason I had no faintest idea—since February of 1942 when I'd met her getting off the evacua-
tion ship in San Francisco. It was true that Colonel
Primrose had been there; he'd introduced us. But that
was because she'd been with a general's wife he knew,
and she introduced Alice to him as I was standing
there. I certainly wasn't there on her account, and
neither, so far as I knew, was Colonel Primrose. Still,
I could easily see why at the moment it might seem
advisable to use us that way, and if any possible connection I had with Colonel Primrose, who was in
Washington the day I left, would help, it was all right
with me. It was all right with me, that is, except when
I remembered that swift terrifying figure in the dark,
and the gleaming knife. He was so right about my not
breathing. I hadn't dared to breathe.

"I'm telling you the truth," Alice Cather repeated.

"All right. I believe you because I have to." The

voice was easy now, all the dark menace gone out of
it. "In any case, my dear, I think you wouldn't try to
lie to me."

It was not till then that I was aware of the shadow
on the floor at the end of the beds. It was motionless
there, a head, a body, elongated from the lanai entrance. I hadn't heard any one coming, and my heart
froze still more. I didn't know what to do. I'd forgotten Mary. I knew it was she, standing there in her
bathing suit, watching me, frozen to the floor, listening
to a conversation from her mother's room, my hat still
on my head. I could almost see the contempt shining
from her clear violet eyes, and there was no way to
explain to her that I had a right to listen. I couldn't
close the door now and turn around. The dark quiet
voice still held me there. If they knew I'd heard . . .
and could still hear, as Roy Cather's voice went on.

"—Because you're in love with me, Alice. You always have been. You've never loved my sainted brother.
If you had——"

I forced myself to turn then. It was Mary, and her
face was pale and intense. She wasn't looking at me,
and she raised her hand quickly to stop me from speaking, and shook her head, listening too.

"If you had, you'd have told Harry this morning
I was back to see him. That's why you came home,
Alice. Because you——"

"That's a lie, Roy! I don't love you—I hate you.
You're simply a fiend——"

The sudden fire of passion in her voice burned across the space between us. Mary had crept in beside me and was holding my arm tightly.

"—A fiend in human form," the man said calmly. "You've gotten dull, Alice. Old and dull, my dear. And you are in love with me—but afraid of me too."

"Of course I'm afraid of you."

Her voice was vibrant with a different kind of passion.

"I can't help myself—there's nothing I can do. But it's not because I love you or because *I'm* afraid of you. It's Mary, and Harry. I'm not going to let you destroy them. That's why I'm bargaining with you— not for myself. I could see you dead and be happier than I've ever been in all my life. And listen to me carefully, Roy. If you get out and stay out, I won't give you up. If you make one move to leave this place before you go for good, I'll . . . I'll tell Harry, and he'll report you. He wouldn't hesitate the way I have. He wouldn't care what happened to any of us. I'm telling you you've got me so far but no farther. I'm like a cornered rat and I'll turn if I have to. You're not going off this place and you're not to use the phone. And *she's* not coming here—I mean that too, Roy. Now go—they'll be coming. I hear the car. Quickly! Not that way . . . here, through her room."

We were simply caught. It's hard now to communicate the acute dismay, and horror isn't too much to say, I think, of the silent message that passed be-

tween the two of us standing there. We were too close
to the door to get away. We couldn't even get into the
bathroom without the sound of the door giving us
away. Mary's hand on my arm was cold as ice, as my
heart was, knowing how silently and swiftly the man
could move. In that brief fraction of an instant he
could be just outside the door. And then we were given
an instant to use. It was Mary who was aware of it
in a flash as his voice came, nearer, terribly nearer it
seemed to me, and so concentrated with its quiet menace
that I'm not sure I'd have had strength to move if it
hadn't been for her.

"Just one thing more, Alice . . ."

We didn't hear what it was. We slipped with a speed
and silence born of awful necessity across the mat-
carpeted floor and out onto the lanai. Suddenly, just
as I thought we were going to make the corner, Mary
drew her breath in with a sharp gasp. Her body went
taut as a bowstring for an instant, and before I knew
what she was doing she was gone, running—running
back the way we'd come. I stared after her with a kind
of incredulous terror. She was at the entrance to my
room again, and inside. I waited, mute with dismay.
It wasn't more than a second, but it was interminable,
before she was out again, running back, white-faced. In
her hand was my bag. I'd left it on the bed, not even
seeing it.

"Quick!" she whispered.

We went faster than that along the lanai to the front

of the house. At the end of the living room she stopped and leaned against the wall, her eyes closed for an instant. When she put her hand out to give me my bag it was trembling.

"That man is a murderer," she whispered. "He . . . he'd have seen it. He'd have known."

We went on till we were at the lanai entrance to her room. I made for the bamboo chaise longue. My knees were too shaky to hold me up any longer.

"No!" she whispered urgently. "Here."

I was conscious of the bathing suit in her hand for the first time. She held it out.

"Put it on in my bathroom, quick, and let's get out. We'll say you stopped here and didn't go to your room. And *I'll* sit down."

She managed to laugh, though it didn't sound the way it was supposed to, sank down in a chair and put her feet up on the ottoman. She let her head fall back and closed her eyes for an instant, but she was getting up as I closed the bathroom door. It seemed a little crazy to me to be madly scrambling into an open midriff bathing suit when I was freezing cold and so shaken I couldn't figure out which was top and which wasn't, but I did it. I was acutely aware that her going back then to get my bag had taken more courage than I would have had, even for myself. I was profoundly grateful to her, realizing what I would have felt, going back and finding it, and from then on waiting, and not knowing. It was bad enough as it was.

When I came out I saw her across the hall standing by a window. She motioned me to come. Through the screen of leafy shrubs we could see the main entrance to the house. Alice was there, looking from our muddy shoes to Kumumato beside her. The car was in the drive. He had obviously been in the process of taking my bags in when she came out. It was equally obvious that they were discussing our present whereabouts.

"She's asking where we are," Mary said.

She was probably doing a lot more than that, I thought, but I didn't say so. It was a little difficult to know whether to tell Mary her precious Kumumato was part and parcel of the whole thing or not. Then, all of a sudden, she said:

"He's in on it too."

She said it quietly, without any surprise or special emphasis.

"—I can tell from here."

How she could, except that her mother was looking back toward her wing and mine and Kumumato was shaking his head, I didn't know, but as she was right it didn't matter very much.

"I'm afraid so," I said.

She stood there, a slim brown mermaid figure in the briefest possible swimming suit, barefooted, her yellow hair tied in an old maid's knot on the top of her head, her face still pale but calm and completely unrevealing. Her mother was turning to come back into the house, and Kumumato was reaching down for our muddy shoes.

She looked around at me. "We'd better go out. Are you game?"

I wasn't, frankly, but she'd been game enough to go back after my bag.

"I'll do my best," I said.

"Okay, let's go. We'll go around the lanai and I'll chatter. Maybe she won't want to see us either. Why do you suppose Kumumato said she wasn't home?"

I'd been wondering about that myself, but I didn't have any idea. It seemed foolish on the face of it, though he wouldn't have any reason to think she wouldn't be able to hear us clattering around.

"I know," Mary said. "We'll go down this way."

She opened a door just before the living-room angle, and we went down a narrow staircase. The service quarters were there and a passage led out onto a tiled strip the width of the lanai above it. There was a small vegetable garden that became lawn and flower garden in front of the living room. A Japanese woman in a gray kimono pulled up to her knees, a big coconut straw hat on her head, was bending over the lettuce heads. She didn't look up as we passed.

"That's the cook, Kumumato's wife," Mary said. "She was a picture bride."

Then she started to chatter. She chattered about the flowers and the dark oriental grass that grew in little hummocks because the roots bunched up under it and you couldn't keep it level. To all visible intents she'd forgotten Uncle Roy existed, while I was listening not to her at all but for her mother's footsteps to come out onto the lanai above us. But they didn't come. We were in the pool, Mary as much at home as a slim silver fish and me lumbering around in comparison, when Alice Cather came out. She called to us gaily and waved her hand. We swam around, and only some minutes later, when we were resting a moment on the broad rim of the pool on the far side did Mary try to speak.

"I don't know what to do," she said, very quietly. "I don't even know what to think. It can't be what it looks like. It *can't.*"

She looked back and up at the rambling house. We could see past the lanai with its pale-gold bamboo chairs and bright-covered cushions into the silvery quiet shadows of the living rooms. It was too civilized and gracious to be a storm center of anything dark and menacing.

"It just *can't* be," she said.

I didn't know what she thought it couldn't be. I had no way of telling what kind of meaning what Roy Cather said to her mother was having to her.

"Grace," she said. "—You don't mind if I call you that, do you?"

I shook my head. She looked back into the deep cleft where the ravine narrowed and the overflow from the pool made a waterfall far down to join the white ribbon of the stream at the bottom, between the great black moss-stained rocks.

"Do you suppose she's fixing the cottage for . . . him?"

I shook my head again. I didn't know anything—and perhaps the less both of us knew the better off we'd be.

She was silent for a moment. Then she slipped down into the crystal water, and I followed her across and out on the grassy terrace under the bank.

The steps to the garden level were a little way from us, but she went along the way the captain and I had gone the evening before. Across the ravine the trees against which I'd seen the apparition that had become all too solid flesh were soft and lovely in the full glow of the afternoon sun streaming in from beyond the edge of the ocean. I was trying to see the face again as I'd seen it in the dusk, and hear the redbird's call, low and now sinister. He must have thought I was Alice Cather, it came to me suddenly, to risk calling and showing himself. And it flashed through my mind then that he must have been closer still to the house to recognize her in my doorway rolling down the curtain, thinking probably it was a signal she was giving him instead of a barrier to close him out from my sight.

We were now almost to the air-raid shelter. Mary was talking, about what I've no idea, but I was acutely conscious suddenly of the quick pressure of her bare wet arm linked in mine.

"Look," she said brightly. "—The sun on the kukui trees. They're the ones with the light green leaves."

She was pointing with her free hand out across the ravine, her arm in mine still warning me with its pressure.

"They always make it look like spring, and when the shower trees are in bloom it's lovely."

I knew then why she wanted me to seem to be looking in the other direction, up toward the sunlit mountain wall. We were just in front of the solid redwood door of the shelter, with its elaborate iron lock and hinges. It was tightly closed, but above it one of the long sprays of orchids had been caught and was held, its petals still crisp and fresh, where the door had closed on it. She must have been seeing in her mind, as I did in mine, the silent figure crouching in the dark behind it, listening to us pass. Only she wouldn't see, as I did, the hand creep back and the long naked blade it held, tense and motionless.

She looked at me, a little pale again, her lips compressed, a startled expression in her eyes. We turned up the steps to the garden level. She was silent the rest of the way back to her room.

Inside she said, "I don't know what to do, Grace. I just don't know. I wish I could talk to her, but I wouldn't dare. She mustn't know we know—not till we know what to do."

Her eyes were bright with sudden tears welling up. "How horrible for her! She must be almost out of her mind, Grace. I feel so dreadfully sorry for her!"

She blinked the tears back quickly.

"And I don't know *what* to do," she repeated, slowly. "The . . . the man back there . . . He's dreadfully wicked. He's horrible, Grace. I . . . I know who he is. And he hates us all, frightfully. They've lived in terror of him for years.—And it's all my fault, I was the one who made her come back. I raised hell till she had to. I wish we'd stayed away!"

"Well, you didn't, angel," I said practically. "There's no use wishing. It won't help, will it?"

She shook her head. "And I've got to do something, and I don't know what . . . and it frightens me. I can't tell you why it does, Grace."

She got up and stood for a moment, listening.

"We've got to hurry. You'll stick by me, won't you . . . I mean, until we *know?*"

I had a kind of fatalistic sinking of the heart, to say the least. Understanding nothing at all, I would stick . . . because I was fairly tightly stuck already, it seemed to me. All I could hope for was that I'd get out without a knife in my back or my throat or wherever. If I weren't just so far from home, I thought. It was all very well for Alice Cather to keep me there under the pretense that I was a secret weapon, of some sort unknown to me, but it did make me unpleasantly vulnerable.

9

A LONG SHAFT OF SUNLIGHT STREAMING IN from the garden, slanting across the tree tops in the valley below us, slanted more sharply and disappeared. I was aware of it with a kind of sick feeling of acute dismay. If I could ever have commanded the sun to stop in its diurnal course, that is the moment I would have done it. The idea of night falling and leaving us remote and isolated in the dense blackout of the brooding mountains was as terrifying as if it had already happened.

Mary came over to me and put her hand on my arm. "Don't be frightened, Grace. He won't hurt you. It's only us. But I . . . I'll bet you wish Colonel Primrose was here, don't you? And why haven't you ever married him . . . or is that not any of my business?"

"Chiefly because he's never asked me to marry him," I said. It was an automatic answer that I'm so used to making, because I'm so often asked whether it's anybody's business, that I didn't have to think. I was trying to think if I did really wish he was there, or was truly thankful he wasn't. In a sense, both. For myself I'd have been delighted. He could have told me what to do. For the girl standing there straight and wide-eyed and pale, in an agony of conflicting doubts and loyalties and with a very real terror in her heart, I was glad he wasn't. She wanted a little time . . . or a little time at any rate was what her mother, apparently, was trying so desperately to play for. I really couldn't think whether I wanted Colonel Primrose there or not, with his black X-Ray eyes that see through subterfuge at once and his uncompromising ruthlessness that wouldn't hesitate one instant if necessary to ruin the Cathers or any one else.

"I don't know," I said. I went into the bathroom and got my clothes.

"I'll go around and use my own shower," I said, and started for the lanai. I turned back as Mary called me. She came quickly over.

"Listen, Grace—I've got to tell you."

Her face had the look of a person's who'd been thinking deeply and determined to come squarely to grips with an unpleasant fact.

"I've been telling you a lie, sort of . . . and I mustn't. The man back there is my Uncle Roy. I told you about him. I don't know how he got here now, or why he's here, but I know one thing—he shouldn't be. He doesn't live in Java, Grace. He lives in Japan. And he was there two months ago. I know he was. There was a broadcast somebody sent to us. He said he'd come, but . . . we thought it was just him trying to get us in trouble."

Her face was very pale, but her words were clear and distinct and orderly.

"I'm not supposed to know any of this. I . . . found out, because Mother was frantic. I couldn't believe it. It isn't *possible*. But it's true, Grace. He has no right to be here—it's . . . terribly wrong. I ought to go and tell my father. You ought to go and call the . . . the Army. And I won't try to stop you. But Grace . . . if you could wait, just till tomorrow morning? If you don't, we're ruined . . . Mother and Dad, I mean. I don't care about myself. But they've never done anything disloyal, to anybody, and it's not right for them to suffer. I'm not asking you to betray anybody. I'll watch tonight. Watch him, and . . . Kumumato."

She stopped for a moment.

"Just till morning, Grace. *Something* is bound to happen."

I didn't know what to say or do.

"Will you, Grace? There's nothing he can do tonight. He can't get out of the shelter. I'll lock it. Please, Grace—will you?"

"I . . . don't know," I said. "I just don't know. I'll have to see."

We heard a gay voice calling. "—Darling?"

Mary's hands clenched tightly and she caught her breath. Alice Cather was coming along the inside hall.

"Hurry," she whispered. She gave me a little shove onto the lanai. I heard her voice behind me, casual and light-hearted. "Yes, Mother.—We had a divine swim . . ."

I went quickly along to my room. My bags were unpacked and my clothes neatly pressed and hung up in the closet. I took a shower and got dressed. I went out on the lanai and came back in again a dozen times, I guess. I did everything I could to delay my final going out into the long silver wood-panelled dining room. I tried to think and I tried not to think. It was the clear and simple truth that my duty was what Mary had said it was, of course. I ought to go and call up G2 at once. There was no doubt of that, none in the least.

And every time I made up my mind that that was what I would do, and do at once, Mary Cather's white face and her wide imploring eyes and the touch of her hand on my arm came back to me, and I could see her barring my way to the door, begging one night's grace for her mother and father. And I could hear Alice Cather again, passionately protective as she'd been the night before, or frantic but determined as she'd been in the afternoon, making up a whole fabric of falsehood as a stopgap against the tide of disaster rising around her.

I stopped for the twentieth time, I suppose, in front of the dressing table, and picked up my comb to do my hair over again. I still didn't know what I was going to do. A light tap on the door made me start sharply. I didn't want to face Alice Cather then, not in the least, but I knew I had to.

"Come in," I called.

It wasn't Alice. It was Kumumato, his face impressive and quite without any expression that I could read. He bowed a little, or ducked his head a little rather. "The telephone, madam," he said. It was the first time I'd heard him speak. I suppose I expected him to use pidgin English, but he didn't. "This way, if you'd like me to show you, madam."

I pulled myself hastily together and started to follow him. The door of Alice Cather's sitting room was partly open, and I heard her voice, so different that it was hardly recognizable as the one I'd listened to earlier.

". . . sure you wouldn't mind, Harry," she was saying, cool and light and completely assured again. "It seemed such a shame to have the cottage just standing . . ."

I was out of earshot then, but it was enough. And Mary was right. As she'd predicted, the guests had arrived before supper. I wondered, as I followed Kumumato's stocky figure along the passage. I wondered whether it was just Aunt Norah she was trying to keep out, or whether the old business of safety in numbers wasn't involved. The more people there were around, the less freedom of action there'd be for the gentleman in the air-raid shelter. It struck me suddenly as rather pathetic, the frail and futile defenses she was using to enforce her end of the grim bargain she'd made. It was like using the ribbon from a hand-painted box of candy to tie up the gate against a rising devastating

flood . . . or saying, "Look, there are some people
in the house by the road, so you can't go out" to a man-
eating tiger who could slip silent and unseen through
the jungle growth of the ravine. I felt very sorry for
her, some way.

In the entrance hall a door balancing the one to the
lower level was open. The telephone receiver was lying
on the table in the little room. I went in and picked
it up, and started to close the door, because I decided
then that it was fate taking me to the telephone in
. spite of myself, and I might as well submit with what
grace I could. I'd have to go out then and tell Alice
Cather and her daughter, but once done it would be
over and a part of my conscience would be clear anyway.
But I didn't close the door. Kumumato was too busy
brushing up something that probably wasn't there, by
the entrance, and I didn't want him listening when
I finally made my own call. I turned around with my
back against the wall where I could see him as well
as be seen by him.

"Hello," I said. I hadn't even wondered who was
calling me.

"You're very difficult to get hold of, Mrs. Latham."

"Colonel Primrose!"

I said it—gasped it is better, I suppose—more as a
general announcement than as recognition of him. For
a moment my heart rose—or fell, I can't say which.
Then as quickly it occurred to me he wasn't there
in Honolulu. It was long distance, probably.

"Where are you?" I demanded.

"I'm at Hickam Field, at the moment," he said. "How are you?"

I remembered Kumumato then and glanced at the door where he'd been. But he was gone.

"I'm fine," I said.

I thought I noticed an instant's hesitation at the other end, and wondered if there'd been anything in my voice.

"I won't keep you then. I'll see you—this evening, perhaps, if you're going to be at home."

I said all right. I don't quite know how I said it, but I did. I heard his laugh as he said, "Good-bye, my dear," and the phone was dead. I stayed where I was for several moments. I had a strange feeling that a blank wall had suddenly risen in front of me.

Yet in a sense it was a sharp relief. If there was any question of whether Roy Cather had come, however he may have come, from Japan or from anywhere off the Island, if Mary was right about what she'd gleaned about his past, then there was no possible compromise. I'd known that really all along. There's duty that's more compelling than friendship or the obligation of a guest in anybody's house. Colonel Primrose would come and I would tell him the story. In my way I guess I was as optimistic as Alice Cather. He hadn't seen me for over two weeks, and it never for an instant occurred to me he'd let anything stand in the way of coming to see me as soon as he could. Which only proves again the profound conceit of the female.

I've pretended for a long time that my friendship with the colonel, who lives with his iron-bound, rock-faced, fishy-eyed Sergeant Buck, once top sergeant and now legman extraordinary in their shadowy liaison with first one and then another of the Intelligence Divisions in Washington, is casual and unimportant, but I think I'd be pretty upset if I really thought so. Whether he actually would want to give up the ease and freedom of fifty-odd years of bachelorhood, I don't know. The idea of his marrying me was certainly at first just a horrible nightmareish figment in his sergeant's mind. Having protected him through the last war from shot and shell and Army rations and nothing but water to drink, it was Sergeant Buck's plain duty to go on protecting him from the designs of the widow across the street. If his methods were as frail and obvious in their way as Alice Cather's seemed to me to be in hers, they had so far succeeded, anyway. I prefer to leave out my side of the case. I've never been quite sure, for example, that Colonel Primrose and Sergeant Buck and I would always see eye to eye about the conduct of my two small boys. My doubts were gravest the day I found them in the area way outside the kitchen with Sergeant Buck teaching them to say "Seven come eleven." I had to give them extra allowance money for Christmas, and the headmaster wrote a tactful letter when they went back to school in January. When you're dealing with the Army there are a lot of things you have to consider, and where Colonel Primrose is his sergeant is sure to be.

However, my problem at the moment was settled, and I came out of the telephone closet with mixed but less fundamentally disturbed emotions. At least I wasn't going to aid and abet the enemy. I looked around to see if Kumumato was still in spying distance, but he was nowhere in sight. I had a vaguely uneasy feeling that if Alice Cather had told Roy Cather about Colonel Primrose, Kumumato might very well know about him too, and perhaps I'd made a mistake in gasping out his name. I began to wish he'd come quickly . . . in fact, before the sun went down.

I shut the door to the closet. I could hear Alice and her husband coming along the hall from her sitting room, talking pleasantly. I might have waited for them to go with me into the living room, but I didn't. I put off the evil moment of having to face her for another few seconds, and started in by myself. And I stopped, stopped as abruptly as blazes, I may say.

"—good deal, eh what, my lads?" I heard. "*Jeepers!* Free rent, laundry collected, luau juice on the house —imported, I hope, direct from Scotland, no local cane squeezings disguised as gin. Oh, boy, is this pretty!"

It was a familiar voice, and the hushed irritated reply was just as familiar.

"Shut up . . . you want to get us thrown out before we're in?"

I went mechanically the rest of the way across the

polished floor of the entrance hall to the broad archway down two steps into the living room. There was no mistake. There they were, Lieutenants Thomas E. Dawson and David Boyer, standing in the middle of the long room, Lieutenant Dawson looking the place over as if about to buy it and send it home as a souvenir.

"Nice little grass shack they've got here, eh, David?"

And that was not all. Swede Ellicott was there too. He was over in the opening onto the lanai, but he wasn't looking the place over. He was standing stock-still, frozen in his tracks, staring down at the other end of the room, his face a complete blank, the cigarette in one hand motionless, the lighter in the other flaring like a large and fitful candle. I looked the way he was staring. Mary was there at the entrance of the passage to her wing. She had stopped as motionless and blank as Swede.

When I said surprise was not the word, that consternation fitted better, it was, I think, an understatement. Even Tommy Dawson, never known to be nonplussed by anything at all, stopped dead when he turned and saw first me and then Mary, his freckled face blanker for an instant than both Swede's and Mary's put together.

Then he said, "Jeepers." He turned to Dave Boyer. "David—I thought you said '*Flather*,' David . . ."

He turned back to us, a sardonic lift to one eyebrow.

"Well, well," he said. "Fancy meeting you girls here. What a small, small world it *really* is, after all."

10

MARY CATHER'S IMPULSE TO TURN AND RUN
was as evident as if she'd already made the initial move.
It wouldn't take a second for Alice Cather to get here
—and that was what I was waiting to see. But before
she came Mary proved she was her mother's own
daughter. She didn't turn and flee and she didn't do
anything crazy that she'd regret the rest of her life.
She raised her chin a little and came forward quickly,
her body very straight, her eyes brighter than they
should have been, probably, and her cheeks warmer.
They only made her look more vivid and really very
lovely.

She held out her hand. "Hello, Tommy—hello,
Dave," she said, as calmly as if she'd left them just
after lunch at the Outrigger Club. "Are you the guests
we're expecting for the cottage?"

She turned then. It must have taken more effort
than all the rest of it.

"Hello, Swede, how are you?"

She smiled and turned back to Tommy. "Won't you
all sit down? Mother's just coming."

Her eyes met mine for an instant. Her look was blank and at the same time oddly communicating. It said, "—Did you know about this?" It said, "What are we going to do now?" and "Where on earth is Mother, why doesn't she come?"

I hadn't said anything. I was aware of the slight jolt to Tommy Dawson's amazing aplomb as he realized their being there was as much of a shock to the little Cather as it was to him and Swede. He was also casting another suspicious sidelong glance at Dave Boyer that underlined his "David—I thought you said *Flather*, David." On the other hand Dave Boyer was completely at ease, or was until he heard Alice in the hall. Swede was the only one who seemed unable to adjust himself with any degree of articulate grace. If he'd said "Hello" or anything else in response to Mary's greeting I for one didn't hear it. He was caught as completely off base as it was possible to imagine, his face an extraordinary picture, flushed and dark, not truculent or sullen but very hard-bitten and unsmiling. And he was unable to take his eyes away from the slim golden-skinned girl in the blue gingham dress with a blue ribbon holding the damp curls back from her forehead. She looked nearer twelve than twenty, but she was as outwardly composed and casual as a woman who'd spent a lifetime coping with unexpected guests.

"What would you like to drink?" she asked. "I'm sure we've got some Scotch—from Scotland."

She smiled at Tommy, who had the grace to blush

to the freckled roots of his ginger-colored hair. And that was when Alice Cather and her husband appeared at the top of the two broad steps leading from the hall into the living room. It was the moment I'd been waiting for. Alice appeared there smiling like any hostess knowing her guests were waiting and she herself a little late, coming in quickly not to keep them waiting longer. And she stopped. For a superb fraction of a second the smile left her face, and left it blankly uncomprehending, for all the world as if instead of the guests she expected she found a troup of orang-outangs in short green pants and boaters. It lasted only an instant—quite long enough to deceive Swede and Tommy, and even Dave for all I knew, and give them the additional jolt that they were as much of a shock to her as she was to them. If it was play-acting it was divine. It didn't look like it even to me, and I saw Mary's startled eyes widen as she pressed the service bell. Then Alice Cather was every inch a hostess again. She came down the steps with a quick light tread, her hand extended.

"This is a very delightful surprise," she said. "We're very lucky. How do you do, Tommy? Harry dear, Lieutenant Dawson, Lieutenant Boyer. Hello, Dave."

She turned and went over to Swede.

"Hello, Swede. It's so nice to see you again. This is Swede Ellicott, Harry. Isn't it pleasant to have people we know in the cottage? I should think you could give them some of your Scotch, darling, to celebrate."

I saw that Harry Cather was a well-trained husband. He plainly had not understood the situation until he heard Swede's name. I thought he stiffened just slightly, and didn't glance at his daughter until he moved aside where he could see her without being obvious about it. His brow was a little clouded, but otherwise he was as always, gentle and reserved and very kindly. I thought again that he was also oddly detached, some way, as if he were also, in a sense, a guest who was pinch-hitting for an absent host. It was probably the effect of never knowing when Aunt Norah would descend.

He went over to the ohia wood cellarette and brought out a bottle of Scotch. Kumumato entered with a tray with glasses and soda and ice, and a cocktail shaker full of daikaris, rum being much less scarce than other forms of what Tommy called luau juice, which except for gas is the only serpent in the otherwise unrationed garden of the paradise of the Pacific.

I can't really think of any particular way to account for the pleasure I was getting out of the discomfiture of Lieutenant Thomas E. Dawson. Finding himself an unexpected guest of the she-buzzard in her own house, he'd suddenly become shy, awkward, heavy-handed and very young, and it was Dave Boyer who was doing the Public Relations job. As for Swede Ellicott, he seemed simply unable to keep from following every move Mary made, with grim unhappy eyes. And she was to all intents unaware he was in the room. The spot where he stood still rooted to the floor might have been empty, or so enchanted that any object on it was totally invisible. She didn't even seem aware of it when he moved abruptly, almost with a wrench, and strode out onto the lanai. Tommy and Dave looked quickly at each other, and Tommy looked at me and made an imperceptible nod toward the opening leading out. I shook my head. I didn't want to go out when Swede obviously must have wanted to be alone a few moments.

And all the time Alice Cather kept up a quiet liquid flow of words that covered everything with a sheen of the best-grade velvet. The second time Tommy looked at me, jerking his head toward the lanai, I went out.

Swede was standing at the corner post, just standing there, his glass still full to the brim, staring out over the treetops not at anything in particular, and not seeing anything either, I imagined, except in his own mind. I didn't want to obtrude, Heaven knew, so I sat myself down on a bamboo chaise longue a little way off. He turned, came over and sat down next to me, his elbows resting on his knees.

He didn't say anything for a minute.

"This your idea, Grace?" he asked then. He was gruff and abrupt to the point of rudeness.

"No," I said. "It was not. It most certainly was not."

"Whose?"

"I've no idea."

"Well, it's lousy," he said. "That situation is over. I'm not back for a second round."

"I don't think any one thinks you are, Swede," I said. "Aren't you taking something a little too much for granted?"

He looked at me quickly, his bleached eyebrows screwed together in a tight straight line, the pupils of his eyes hard black points in a field of blue unrelenting ice. I couldn't tell whether here was a boy who had been hurt too much or just one who thought he was being pushed around. He was one I certainly didn't know, and very different indeed from the boy who'd visited his aunt next door from time to time as he grew up and that I thought I knew fairly well.

"Get this, Grace," he said deliberately. "Since it's come up.—I'm going to marry Corinne. Neither Dawson nor Boyer nor you nor anybody is going to stop me. Get it straight, lady. That's the deal. You can all take it and like it. Corinne's had a rotten deal all her life. It's not her fault her parents weren't the same race. It wouldn't make any difference to me if they were both Hottentots. That's just to get the record straight. And leave us not make any more mistakes about it."

"—Leave us not make any mistakes at all, Swede," I said. I was pretty mad myself at this point. "Suppose you just get something yourself. I don't care who you marry, Corinne, a Hottentot or the Queen of the Esquimaux. I think you're a damn fool—for the record —and you do too, or you wouldn't be on the defensive so. But that's your business. It isn't mine. What is mine

and what I want you to get perfectly straight is this
—I had nothing whatsoever to do with your being
invited here, if you were particularly invited. I didn't
tell Mary you were in Honolulu. I was careful not to
tell her, in fact. I didn't know you were coming here
and neither did she. And you don't have to stay. You
can leave right now or half an hour ago. But quit acting
this way. Nobody says you can't marry Corinne."

"So you're telling me," he said abruptly. "You're
telling me after the royal brush-off I got——"

"Brush-off?" I said.

Tommy Dawson came out onto the lanai.

"What goes on?" he demanded.

Whether it was the luau juice or whether a glass
of water and a little time would have had the same
effect I don't know, but he was himself again, debonair
and everything under control again, taking the place
over for the greater comfort of personnel present of
the United States Army Air Forces of the Pacific Ocean
Area.

"This way, folks, the grand tour starts on your——"

He broke off and looked at Swede, his face sobering
abruptly. He looked at me, and back at Swede. "Or
do you want to stay put?" he said. "Mary's going to
show us around this rugged foxhole of hers. She's just
gone to turn on the lights at the pool."

I got up instantly. The unexpected presence of the
three boys had wiped Uncle Roy completely out of
my mind. He was back again in a flash. The rugged

foxhole he was in under the orchid-covered bank was too near the pool for a grand tour to skip. I thought for an instant Mary might have forgotten. Tommy's nose would be poked in there in nothing flat.

Swede got up, slowly and with deliberation. "I'm shoving," he said calmly.

"Suit yourself." Tommy turned and went back into the living room. I followed him. Swede went over to the rail and stood there again where he'd been when I came out, looking down over the dark slope of wooded hills to the city and to the ocean stretching into the quiet infinity of the far horizon.

Mary wasn't in the room. Dave Boyer was saying to Harry Cather, ". . . B-29 Punch. You take one quart of gin, one quart of rhum, one can of grapefruit juice, one can of pineapple juice, ice if possible but it's not customary . . ."

"It sounds horrible," Alice Cather said, shuddering a little. She looked suddenly pale and distrait. Her eyes were fixed anxiously at the end of the room where Mary was coming back from along the passage from her bedroom wing.

"That's known as gross understatement," Tommy said cheerfully, heading off to join Mary. Swede was the forgotten man. "Come on, David. Coming, Grace?"

Alice Cather made a small frantic movement with her hands.

"Darling, why don't you wait?" She managed to keep her voice casual. "Dinner's almost ready. Harry, do give them another drink and let's all relax. The boys have seen hundreds of swimming pools."

"Well, they're going to see another one right now," Mary said blithely. "We won't be a minute, Mother, and you oughtn't to encourage them to drink anyway. It wrecks their livers. We'll be right back."

I saw there was only one thing Alice Cather could do. It was impossible to forbid them to go, and yet she couldn't let them go in there where I knew Roy Cather was waiting.

"All right, then, dear," she said. "But please don't go into the shelter tonight. I've got a lot of things stuck in there. You can show them that tomorrow."

"Okay, dear," Mary said.

The impulse in Alice Cather to repeat it and insist she be taken seriously must have been as great then as the impulse to go along to see she was obeyed. She took a step or two toward the hall, and caught herself. She went quietly back and sat down.

"Do hurry, then, won't you, darling?"

Mary switched the pool lights on from the panel in the game room where the bamboo bar was, downstairs. It flooded the whole garden and stretched out over the ravine to the high light green of the kukui trees against which I'd seen the disembodied face the night before. I could see it again, more sinister in its meaning now it was crouching, not disembodied, close to us just under the green lawn in front of us. He would have seen the light too, and be waiting.

"Just a second," Mary said. She ran across the room and opened the door into the service quarters. "I'll be right with you."

As she closed the door Dave Boyer turned quickly. "—What happened to Swede?"

Tommy shook his head.

"No soap." He shook his head again. "Didn't work, David. He's not staying. Let's give up. It's his hell. Let him write his ticket there and back. It's what he's going to do anyway."

He was keeping one eye on the door, waiting for Mary to come back.

Dave Boyer grinned lopsidedly. "Oh, yeah?"

"There you go," Tommy said airily, but he reddened to the roots of his hair. "Dawson, the man nobody understands. Ah, Fate! Ah, Life! Ah . . . Mary!"

She was back, a little breathless, closing the door quickly behind her as if she was afraid something was at her heels. The bright spots burned in her cheeks again.

"Come along—we *will* be late," she said.

What had happened and was happening I didn't know, but we'd no sooner got out onto the grass than I heard the door open and Kumumato come out into the game room. For anybody busily getting dinner up to the dining room floor he seemed to have an amazing lot of time to waste. He came on over to the tiled terrace just outside the room, not apparently concerned with us but where he could see us, certainly. I thought

Mary hadn't heard him. She gave no indication of it until we'd crossed the lawn to the stairs going down, not those by the pool but the other ones, to the house side of the air-raid shelter. Tommy was at her side and Dave was with me, that odd grin still hovering in the neighborhood of his dark eyes. He shook his head, nodding at him.

"What a guy," he said.

Tommy Dawson was pointing to a monkey-pod tree, asking Mary if it was an elm. We were just at the top of the stone steps. Mary turned around.

"Oh Kumumato san," she called across to the man on the terrace. "Please go to Dad's study and get me that book on trees for Lieutenant Dawson. It's on the table by the window. Bring it to me here, please."

She smiled over at him, but it was a very surface smile, and I could see a determined gleam in her eyes. She'd known all the time Kumumato was there and she must have been wondering how she was going to get rid of him. Why, I didn't at the moment quite know. And it seemed to me for some reason that the Japanese house man was equally determined not to go. He hesitated very plainly, and Tommy Dawson, about as much interested in trees as in books, came hastily to his aid.

"Oh, don't bother on my account——"

"Not at all," Mary said quickly. "If you're interested . . . Hurry, please, Kumumato—we'll wait."

I thought his position was curiously not unlike Alice

Cather's: he simply couldn't refuse, much as he apparently wanted to. He stood there, however, for another full instant, his face entirely impassive and expressionless, before he said, "Yes, miss," and went.

11

"THE ORCHIDS ARE LOVELY DOWN HERE," Mary said, starting along the minute he was out of sight.

I glanced up at the lanai. It was Alice Cather I was looking for, wondering if her self-control would extend to the point of not letting herself come out up there and watch us too, or if she was depending on Kumumato down below. Whichever it was, she wasn't in sight. Even in the dim glow cast on the lanai from within the house or reflected up from the flood light on the garden, the bulky figure watching us couldn't be mistaken for hers.

It was Swede Ellicott. He was still up there where I'd left him, but he wasn't looking makai any longer. He was looking mauka, though not at the mountains. He turned and stood watching us as we went down the steps.

"—He hasn't gone, after all," I thought.

"—It used to break my heart, on the Mainland," Mary was saying brightly, "when somebody would send me one of those awful sickish lavender cataleyas. They *cost* so much, and nobody ever looks at one out here. Now here's a cataleya that's a beauty."

She went along the grass to the bank, near the air-raid shelter door—so dangerously near that my heart missed a beat, I'm sure—and reached up. She held up a great lovely bloom, its fringed petals white shading to pale lemon.

"But it's these I love." She went a step closer to that redwood door and broke off a cluster of waxen white flowers that looked like a couple of dozen butterfly forms, their wings spread to take off.

"—And this is the shelter we're not to go in," she said very coolly. She raised her voice a little. My eyes were glued to that door. It was closed tight. The spray of orchids caught in the top of it when it was closed the last time was still there, not as fresh as it had been, the mangled petals drooping.

"Let's just take a quick look-see," Tommy Dawson said.

She looked around at him with a quick smile. "Later maybe," she said. And then so quickly and accurately that I was unaware what she was doing until she did it, she thrust a key into the wrought-iron lock and turned it. A bolt clicked home.

She moved on as calmly as if she'd just turned the key on a recalcitrant kitten in the pantry cupboard. Only her arm trembling a little as she put it through mine while we were walking along toward the pool indicated she knew it wasn't any kitten but a man-

eating tiger. And I suppose she was wondering what
to do from then out. I was, certainly. Roy Cather
was locked up for the moment, but moments have a
grim way of being awfully fleeting. It was hard to
believe that a man who wouldn't stick at what Uncle
Roy must have gone through to get across the Pacific
Ocean—coming from where he did—would be stymied
very long by an ornamental wrought-iron door lock.
It was even more disturbing too, because he now knew,
of course, that Mary at least knew he was there.

"—This is the pool," Mary said calmly. "You can
come down the path from the cottage." She pointed
back the way we'd come and around her mother's wing.
"Come any time you want to."

"This is swell," Tommy said. "What time do you
go in?"

"Any time you'd like."

She smiled at him and started up the steps to the
garden level. She still had hold of my arm. As we
got to the top Kumumato was coming through the
service quarters door into the game room with a large
volume in his hand.

Mary laughed.

"There you are, Tommy. You won't have time to
swim."

She took her arm out of mine. "Come on, Grace,
we've got to hurry."

When she took hold of my hand I thought it was
to draw me along faster. When she let go of it I had

in it not a key to the air-raid shelter, I had two keys.
She was putting both hands out for the book.

"—Thank you," she said.

I don't know enough about orientals to know what
Kumumato was thinking. So far as I could see he wasn't
thinking anything. He handed her the book. Then,
instead of going back the way he'd come, he stopped
inside the game room.

"Are you through with the lights, Miss Mary?"

"Yes, thank you."

He clicked the wall switch. The pool and garden
disappeared in a blur of velvety black. He waited
until we went up the stairs, and switched off the game-
room lights too. At the top of the stairs I opened the
bag I was carrying looped around my wrist and slipped
the two keys into it.

Alice Cather put down the evening paper as we came
into the living room. She wasn't distrait or anxious any
longer. She'd cleared one frantic hurdle . . . or none
of us would be there as cheerfully as we were, I imagine
she was thinking as she looked up at us.

"Swede couldn't stay for dinner," she said pleasantly.
"He had an engagement in town. If the rest of you
are ready . . ."

Neither Tommy nor Dave looked at the other.
Mary's face was as orientally blank in its way as Kumumato's had been in its. I was not at the moment interested either in Swede or in dinner. It was myself as
Keeper of the Keys that I was concerned about. I was

rather more than afraid that Mary's collecting them up in her wing and in that brief sortie into the service quarters was as transparent now to me as her thrusting them into my hands had no doubt been to Kumumato. It was just more of the naïve attempt, it seemed to me, to catch a killer shark with a net made of spider web . . . and probably equally futile unless we could somehow keep it in *status quo* until Colonel Primrose got there.

I was wishing desperately, as we sat down, that he'd hurry. The phone ringing just then seemed almost an answer to a prayer. I was sure it was him. But it wasn't. It wasn't anybody.

"—The wrong number, madam," Kumumato said, coming back.

It rang twice more before dinner and once while we were having coffee on the lanai. Each time it was the wrong number, Kumumato said. The last time Alice Cather frowned slightly.

"If it rings again, I'll answer it, Kumumato," she said.

But it didn't ring again, and about ten o'clock, when Harry Cather went to it to make a call himself it was dead.

"Those silly girls," he said patiently.

He shook his head.

"They're always talking to their boy friends and leaving the switch off."

He went to the service door and opened it. "Ku-

mu——," he began, and stopped. The house man was
there. Mary glanced quickly at me and at the bag in
my lap. If the man had been eavesdropping, however,
it had been a waste of time, unless the good-natured
wrangle about whether Tommy was playing bridge or
poker was of any value to him.

"The phone is off somewhere," Harry Cather said.
"Ask the girls to be more careful."

The idea of the two little maids who padded softly
around the table in their white stocking feet and blue
kimonos having a private life and giggling to their
boy friends over the phone was a little startling. They
looked so much like dolls I suppose I'd thought of
them as automatons. I could see them now giggling
and ducking off, probably when Kumumato appeared,
in their haste disrupting the communications system of
the entire house. Colonel Primrose, however, might
have tried to call. I glanced at my watch. It was too
late for him to come now, I thought unhappily, as
Tommy and Dave were getting up to go. Alice Cather
was doing nothing to detain them. I didn't want them
to go at all. I felt very much as I had when the sun
was making his final bow at the curtain of the day. It
meant we'd be alone. And I'd have to go back to that
open-work room of mine. In any case, lock or no lock
Roy Cather was much too close. I took a tight hold
for a moment on the keys in my bag, knowing all the
time I had no real faith in them.

It was Tommy's idea that we walk up to the cottage

with them. I suppose my instant acquiescence was another frail attempt at a delaying action. Mary's reason
for deciding it would be fun if her mother went along
too might have been two-sided, but Alice's rather surprising agreement—so they could show them the back
path to the pool, she said—seemed nothing more than
a desire to get them home as quickly as she could.
When we started, the light bouncing along the white
coral ribbon of the lane under the bank didn't help a
great deal. I kept hearing the pad of jungle feet creeping behind us in the dark . . . in spite of the keys.
My heart contracted with sickening panic at every bend
in the road. It was a terrific relief when we were in
the cottage at last and the lights were on.

"—Disorderly beggars, your guests."

Tommy looked at the bags open on the floor through
the door of the bedroom. At least two of them were.
The third marked with Swede Ellicott's initials was
neatly strapped up and sitting over by the front door
of the small living room. Tommy and Dave glanced
at it and away quickly. In the fireplace was a scattered
litter of wadded-up sheets of blue writing paper from
the desk in the corner. If Swede had been there in
person, packing up or sitting, chewing the end of his
pen, trying to write a note or explanation, apology,
farewell or whatever, it couldn't have been clearer.
There was no finished note on the desk or the mantel,
however, and the bag at the door seemed to say that
he'd tried to go but couldn't. If any one of us saw it

and it was what they had come to see, nobody said so.

"I think you'll be comfortable," Alice Cather said. "You can have breakfast at the pool, or cook it here yourselves if you'd rather."

She held out her hand. "We must go now, and you're not coming with us. You're staying here and going to bed. Come along, you two. We'll go back the front way."

That was a terrific relief too. I didn't want to do that lane again. At the end of the path we turned and waved to the two tall lean figures outlined against the light from the living room.—They, I thought suddenly, were in for the night.

Alice put the flashlight on for us to see our way in to the drive. Mary stopped abruptly, looking toward the gate.

"Who's that, Mother?"

It was so black under the wide fringe of jungle growth of trees there in the rain-drenched woods that it was hardly possible to see at all.

"It looked like a car, when your light was on. Here —let me have it."

She took the flash from her mother's hand and pressed it on. At the end of the misty triangle of light spreading toward the gate was a black coupé, its head-lights staring like two blind white eyes as they picked up and reflected our light back to us.

"It's probably just somebody parked," Alice said. "We ought to lock the gates at night."

"But there's nobody in it." Mary still held the car centered in the frail beam.

"I know, darling," her mother said patiently. "I wouldn't investigate, if I were you. Come on."

The girl turned reluctantly.

"I wish we had some dogs," she said. "I don't see why Kumumato's so dead set against them. They wouldn't hurt the orchids . . ."

Her voice trailed off as if, I thought, she'd already answered that and was only going on mechanically. It must have been an old controversy, as her mother didn't bother to answer. We went on in silence.

It seemed strange to me, thinking it over, that it was Mary and not her mother who was uneasy about that empty car. If Mary was so convinced her prisoner was locked up . . . Alice Cather had made it one of the conditions of her "bargain" that Roy Cather would not try to leave the place until he left for good and all. It seemed odd that she thought she could trust him, and that she wasn't instantly alarmed at the sight of a car so close to his hideout. But she wasn't in the least, apparently. And I still had those keys in my bag.

12

IF THERE WAS EVER A TIME WHEN THE GIFT
of premonition that both Mary and her mother seemed
to think they'd imbibed from the Island's atmosphere
of brooding mystery, a sort of Hawaiian contagion,
would have been useful, that was it right then as we
were on our way back to the house. It may be that
Mary's uneasiness was something of the kind, and that
her mother's practical realism dissolved it, as practical
realism has a way of doing to premonitions generally.
Anyway, I've often wondered what they would have
thought—or I would have thought—if Mary had thrown
the beam of the light over under the spreading monkey-
pod tree just then and seen Corinne Farrell stop at
Swede Ellicott's side, breathlessly, her hand on his
arm, waiting for us to pass and go on into the house.
I've wondered what we would have thought, guessing
as we no doubt would have done correctly then, that
his bag at the door was far from a sign of indecision
. . . that it was just waiting there fully packed, to
be picked up and put in Corinne Farrell's car at the
gate. It was a second escape for Mary from seeing them

together. I'm not sure if I'd been aware of it myself
I wouldn't have had a premonition of my own. Blind
chance might save her once, but it could only be Fate
saving her a second time . . . and not because of kind-
ness, but because the blow preparing and waiting in
the rather grim stage we were treading wasn't ready
yet in all its devastating fullness. It was like Corinne
and Swede just then, invisible in the dark periphery
of the path toward home.

I don't remember that I've ever wanted less to go
to any room than I did to go to mine that night, or
known less how to get around it. There was no getting
around it, in fact. The lights in the living room were
off and the place settled for the night. Harry Cather
had gone to his study, and Kumumato was in there
with him, leaning over the desk. They were going over
accounts, I imagined. We'd seen them through the
leaves as we came into the courtyard.

"Good night, Mary." Her mother dismissed her
with a light kiss. Alice and I were left alone—me still
with the keys. There'd been no chance for Mary to
take them or for me to try to decide what was best
to do with them.

At the end of the passage Alice opened my door and
switched on the lights for me.

"Good night, Grace."

She hesitated, undecided and rather anxious-eyed.
As well she might be, I thought. For all she knew her
precious brother-in-law might easily decide to take an-

other nocturnal prowl for checking-up purposes. If he believed her story about my status as a Colonel Primrose stooge and stool-pigeon, she must realize how slender the thread was that my life hung on just then. I knew she didn't trust Roy Cather any farther than he trusted her. I had an odd feeling standing there: I didn't know whether to be grateful for her anxiety and indecision, or to admire the fortitude with which she was leaving me, for all she knew, to get my throat cut. I thought that glibly enough then, without myself actually realizing how ghastly near the truth it was, and that without actually meaning to, it was in point of fact precisely what she was deciding.

"Good night," she said again. She closed the door. I heard her cross the passage and close the door of her sitting room. Then there was silence, profound, penetrating and alive the instant it descended. I felt as if I had a sense of trapped dismay crawling up and down my spinal column.

I looked out onto the lanai and across the black void that was the garden under me to the deeper black of the mountains looming up beyond the ravine. My dismay sharpened acutely as I realized I might as well be standing in the center of a brightly lighted stage. There was no audience, I hoped, except leaves and trees and solid rock—as long as Roy Cather stayed underground anyway—but I had the feeling of being watched by a thousand silent hidden eyes. I turned out the light, turned it out as quickly as I possibly could.

For a moment the darkness had a pleasant quality of safety. I felt my way over to the dressing table, put my bag with the keys to Roy Cather's prison down on it and sat down to get my eyes used to the absence of light. I don't know what there is about darkness and silence that makes one listen so intently, unless it's something out of all our primeval past, but I was listening with almost painful intensity. Or perhaps my inner ear had already caught the quiet sound of footsteps on the lanai matting.

I waited, holding my breath, and then let it go abruptly with profound relief. It was Mary. Her figure was outlined against the star-lit night as she stopped at the rail for an instant, looking down into the garden.

She turned and crept into my room.

"Here I am," I said.

"Sssh." She touched my shoulder in the dark. "Come on in here."

It was the strangest conference I've ever been a member of. We closed the bathroom door, turned on the light and sat side by side on the slippery edge of the green-enamelled tub, the drip-drip-drip of a defective shower head behind us punctuating our hushed talk with a kind of ominous persistence.

"Kumumato knows I've got his keys," she said softly. "There are just the two—Dad's and the one in the pantry for the servants. He can't get out. It's a special lock. The wood's only a facing—the door's off an old safe from the office. It locks automatically when the bolt slips and makes the place blast-proof. That's why Dad used it—it's very fancy. So he's *in* all right. The question is, what do we do next?"

"Right," I said.

She looked up at the dripping shower. There was something frustrating and drearily hopeless about the sound of it. She got up abruptly, tried to turn it off and made it worse. She sat down again with a shrug.

"Listen," she said, very quietly. "You'll be furious with me, but I . . . I listened in on your phone call from Colonel Primrose. In Dad's study. I didn't mean to, really, at first, and only for a minute. Just long enough to——"

"That's all right," I said.

"It's not, really, of course. I was hoping it was him. It just sort of popped into my mind when I heard him ask for you that it was him maybe.—Where is he? Isn't he coming out to see you?"

"I thought he would," I said.

"I thought so too. That's why I locked him in. I thought Colonel Primrose could . . . sort of take over for us. I thought he'd be decent about it—for Mother and Dad, I mean."

She hesitated. "He would be, wouldn't he, Grace?"

She looked so pathetically in earnest that I didn't have the heart to tell her the truth.

"As decent as he could be, I guess."

Even that was wishful thinking on my part, knowing as I did that decency is a very relative term in the grim business Colonel Primrose is in. What she'd think

was decent would probably be what he'd regard as a
complete betrayal of his duty. However . . .

"It's the only thing to do," she said practically.
"There's nothing else. We'll just have to take it, that's
all. It's ghastly, but that's the way it is."

There's a kind of realism in the young that's very
moving. Hers was to me then. I don't think she would
have acted differently if she'd known what she was
actually doing, to herself as well as the others.

"So, we'll keep him locked up tonight, and we'll get
Colonel Primrose in the morning. I'll . . . have to
tell Mother, I guess. After we get hold of him."

She got up.

"Where are the keys? I don't want you to be responsible for them."

"They're in my bag, on the dressing table."

"I'll just leave them there, then. It's a better place
than in my room."

She put her hand on the glass door knob and paused.

"Do you think . . . Swede's going to come back—
to stay?"

She asked it without turning her head.

"I think so," I said.

"What's the matter with the other two? What are
they so worried about him for? Are they . . . are they
afraid he's going to fall in love with me again?"

That was definitely a question I didn't want to answer. I said, "It looks to me as if Tommy has already
done that himself, hasn't he?"

She looked at me quickly then, her face suddenly

lighting with that spontaneous laughter of hers that she must have learned, some way, from living up there where the sun could shine brilliantly ten feet from where it was pouring black clouds of rain.

"That's the game I know about now," she said. "I've got the ground rules this time. And he's really fun, isn't he?"

"Just be sure he's got the ground rules too, won't you, angel?" I said smiling.

She laughed softly and turned off the light before she opened the door and slipped out. I heard her brush against the stool in front of the dressing table and the sound of my bag being picked up off the glass top before she went lightly across the room out onto the lanai. Or I assumed she'd gone out that way. I closed the door, turned the light on again, washed my face and got ready for bed, struggled for a moment with the shower and ended by putting the bath mat under it to deaden the drip.

When I went back into the room the door into the passage was open a little, not shut the way Alice Cather had firmly left it. The instant alarm I felt I managed to put aside, realizing that Mary had no doubt gone that way instead of the other. I managed to put it aside, but there must have been a large residue of it left, for I couldn't help opening the door farther and looking out into the passage. It was dark as pitch. There wasn't even a line of light under Alice Cather's door. That may have had some connection with the sudden impulse I had too. But I think my conscience was more deeply concerned then. I was suddenly acutely worried. If anything did happen, it was going to be very difficult to explain the facts to Colonel Primrose without looking precariously like an accessory after the fact.

And the fact that I already was, of course, made it seem more imperative that I get in touch with him at once, by hook or crook. There was no point in calmly waiting until morning.

I looked at my clock on the table between the beds. The illuminated hands stood at twenty-five minutes past twelve. He should be wherever he was staying by this time, and there were only three hotels he was likely to be at. That must have decided me, I think, because I didn't stop to think any more about it. I slipped as quietly as I could out of the door and down the passage to the phone in the entrance hall. I didn't turn on the light to look up the phone numbers. It was easier to get them from Information.

I took down the phone and waited. Nothing happened. There was nothing but the blank hollow sound that comes with a disconnected telephone. That was all. The phone was dead as a door nail. And it couldn't be the little maids and the boy friends again. I was not only convinced of that; I was convinced it hadn't ever been the little maids at all. It was somebody who didn't want the telephone to ring . . . or didn't want any one in the house calling any one outside. It was simply a technique of modern warfare, the disruption of communications, and it was as effective on this small scale as on a larger.

I put the phone down and sat there in the dark wishing . . . wishing first that I had never set foot in Honolulu, T. H., and second that I was back in my own room without having to get there. It's always so much easier to go some place under a sudden impulse than it is to get back again.

In this instance, however, the difficulty was after I'd got back. Alice Cather's light was on, this time, and as I reached my door she opened hers. She had on a light wool robe but she hadn't been in bed. Her hair was still neatly waved and her lipstick hadn't been washed off.

"Darling!" she exclaimed. "What on earth! What are you prowling around at this time of night for?"

It may have been the way she said it, I suppose, or no doubt it was for some reason quite irrational. But I was suddenly annoyed and irritated beyond endurance. It may have been pure frustration, but I didn't stop to think of that. I was just plain mad as hops.

"Look, Alice," I said. "Let's stop all this nonsense. It's simply stupid. I'm prowling around because I went to the telephone to call Colonel Primrose."

In the oblique light from the sitting room I saw her lips tighten.

"Oh, really?" she said. "Is . . . Colonel Primrose——"

"Yes, he is," I said. "But your phone's dead again."

Her eyes lighted with relief.

"The maids, probably. They're so silly."

"Rot," I said sharply. "The phone is cut off on purpose."

"*On purpose?* Darling, what is the matter with you?"

There was not a flaw in the smoothly lacquered surface. That made me angrier still, and I did something that I suppose I should never, never in the world have done.

"There is nothing the matter with me, Alice," I said deliberately. "And there's no use of playing this crazy game a minute longer. I did see your prowler, as you call him, last night. He got my room mixed up with yours . . . as you know . . . and he nearly scared the daylights out of me. And he still does. And I know he's in the air-raid shelter right now——"

"Oh, Grace!" she said.

Her voice and manner were perfect, I suppose. The voice had the weary patience of a martyred saint dealing with a disturbed but harmless schizophrenic.

"Darling, what *are* you talking about? I told you about my prowler because I was afraid you might have waked and been alarmed. But I assure you, my dear Grace, he's not here now. There is *nobody* in the air-raid shelter . . . nobody at all! You're just tired and overwrought, darling."

If she hadn't said that last I might possibly have had the coolness to have pretended I believed what she'd said before. But the tired and overwrought gambit was to me and has always been a very, very red flag to a frenzied bull.

I suppose I absolutely snapped at her, I was so furious.

"We'll see in the morning . . . he's locked in for the night!"

She had turned a little at the first, shrugging her shoulders, agreeing that in the morning we would see. Then she stopped. She didn't stop all at once. It was as though the stopping was taking place nerve by nerve and muscle by muscle, in a delayed, creeping traumatic shock.

"*Locked?*"

I saw her lips move, but the sound from them was barely audible even across the tiny passage.

Her eyes widened with a sudden frantic realization of what I'd really said.

"Not locked, Grace," she whispered.

"Locked," I said. "With a key."

Her hands, shaking as if they were palsied, crept to her throat.

"Oh, my God," she whispered.

She really couldn't speak at all for an instant. Then she said, again so I could barely hear her, "Oh, my God! The phone . . . *the telephone.*"

Her face was terrible. It wasn't white, or gray. It was an awful pale ghastly green. She tried to move, staggering a step or two down the passage, before she crumpled silently on the floor.

13

THE FIRST-AID TRAINING I TOOK AT THE
beginning of the war was so spotty I've always been
thankful I was never called on to use it. I managed,
though, to get Alice onto my bed and get her feet
higher than her head and some cold water on her face,
but mostly on her hair and the silk blanket spread.
I was pretty unnerved myself and in a minor state of
shock—from dismay at my own stupidity as much as
anything. As soon as I could leave her I was going
to dash over to the other wing and get Mary. But I
didn't have a chance. Almost as if she was aware of
what was in my mind, and before I'd have thought
she was really conscious, she caught my hand.

"Don't go," she whispered. She moved her head
weakly from side to side. "I can't stand it, Grace. I
can't *bear* it."

She kept moving her body as if she were in actual
physical pain as well as emotional. And I felt like a
dog. If only I'd had sense enough to keep my mouth
shut! Still, I told myself, it was a shock that was bound

to come. It would have been just as bad in the morning with Colonel Primrose's coming.

"You don't understand," she whispered. "Oh, dear, what shall I do—what shall I do?"

It seemed to me I sat there with her a very long time. The grip of her hand tightened after a while. She was trying to think. As Mary had said, you could always tell. There was a kind of inner concentration that was plainly visible on her face even with her eyes closed. I only wished I could go farther and read what it was she was thinking, but I couldn't. And I wouldn't have dared to try to guess.

She drew herself up then and sat with her body against the headboard.

"Listen, Grace."

It was an impulse of weakness, I suppose, that quivered for an uncertain moment on the threshold of her mind before she controlled it. And control it she did.

"You wouldn't understand. You'll . . . just have to wait, and forgive me if you can."

She shook her head abruptly then and blinked her eyes.

"For Heaven's sake," she said, very much if not entirely like her old self again. "What *is* the matter with me? What happened? Did my heart act up again? I should have warned you. It always frightens me too —I get hysterical."

"Okay, dear," I said. I got up, and this time she made no move to stop me. If that was the story, as fantastic in its way as the one about the GI from the jungle training center on the windward side of the Island was in its, I was in no mood to argue.

She got up and came unsteadily to where I was standing by the dressing table, and put her hand on my arm.

"You terrified me for a moment, Grace. The idea of that poor child being locked up in the shelter is awful. He'd smother to death in the first place, and if Harry finds it out and reports him, goodness only knows what they'll do to him. How long has he been there?"

"I wouldn't know," I said. I really had no idea of what to say.

"You look exhausted, dear, and I know I am. I must get to bed. Do get some sleep. I tell you, Grace, you're simply imagining things . . . but we'll certainly get in touch with Colonel Primrose the first thing in the morning, as soon as it's light, and let him look around. I knew they'd been all over the hills, the last few days, looking for somebody. It never occurred to me for an instant it might be that poor boy. I thought some civilian might have got lost. Didn't you see the planes yesterday? They were flying very low, and there were several details around the Pali."

I was thinking of the day before. The planes Swede had spotted were searching planes. I thought of the evasive answer the officer had given me on the Pali, and wondered if it could conceivably be Roy Cather they were hunting. But if they knew some one had come stealthily on the Island, it would be a Japanese they would be hunting, and in the caves and the oriental districts. They wouldn't be expecting a traitor of their own blood.

"Now go to bed, Grace—you really distress me."

She was herself again except for the pallor she couldn't control by sheer will power.

"If he really is locked up," she said calmly, "and isn't smothered, we'll turn him over to Colonel Primrose. Or I'll call G2. Now relax and go to sleep, angel."

I didn't go to sleep, when she left, and I didn't relax, for that matter. I didn't know what I was going to do, except that I was going to wait and telephone Colonel Primrose if it was the last thing I ever did. Also, I was going to keep an eye on that air-raid shelter so that if she and Kumumato had a way of letting him out that Mary didn't know about, they'd see me sitting like a death's head up on the lanai watching them. How I expected to do both at the same time I wasn't sure.

I was confident of Mary, that she was telling the truth about there being only two keys, and that she wouldn't under any pressure turn them over to her mother. I had no doubt that her mother would bring such pressure. Obviously if the shelter was locked it could only have been done by either Mary or Harry Cather, and she could dismiss her husband at once,

knowing it was Mary who had been with me outside
after Roy Cather left her and returned to his hand-
made cave under the garden. Harry Cather was completely out of it, as remote and detached, in fact, as
he was in spirits when he moved around the house,
as if in it but not entirely of it, as I'd already thought
of him.

I put a quilt around my shoulders, turned off the
light again and went out on the lanai. It was quite
cold for the sub-tropics, and dark except the sky that
seemed almost light in contrast with the blackness of
the ravine and the mountain range stretching off into
the distance. I wrapped the quilt around me, my eyes
gradually accustoming themselves to the dark and the
outlines of the garden and pool and steps, and sat down
on the bamboo chaise longue to keep a childish vigil.
And I kept it. I was disturbed only once. That was
when Alice Cather came back to my door inside.

"Grace darling," she said. "It isn't the maids. The
phones are all on, the pantry and the hall, the one
in Harry's study and mine. It's something else, outside
—probably a branch across a wire. We'll report it in
the morning."

She didn't come into the room or seem to notice
that my "Okay, dear," came from out on the lanai.
She said good night again and closed the door. I didn't
bother to move, as obviously there was no use. It was
a stalemate all around—I trusted. I couldn't move that
way and I hoped she realized, being a bright woman,

that she couldn't move the other, with me sitting out there.

And I sat there until it was light. I was not asleep at any time, and in the overwhelming silence, broken only by the quiet drone of a group of Black Widow night fighters overhead, I would have thought I'd have heard any one coming to the house if they'd come normally at all. And yet the first person I saw as I went around the lanai to breakfast—unwilling and embarrassed after what had happened, I hardly need to say—was Norah Bronson. She was sitting at the table with the Cathers as rigid and unprepossessing as ever, but very obviously a guest who had spent the night and just got up. For an instant I couldn't believe I was seeing straight.

"Good morning, Grace—sit right here by Norah."

Alice smiled up at me as if nothing at all had ever happened to embarrass either of us remotely and as if Aunt Norah had been there all the time. I couldn't have been more flabbergasted if Uncle Roy had been there. I looked at Mary. Her face was a little pale and tight but perfectly blank, and her eyes were blank too. There was no visible change in Harry Cather as he put his paper down and smiled good morning to me. Aunt Norah gave me a brisk nod. Kumumato serving from a side table looked precisely as always. The only thing I could think of was that I'd completely lost my mind.

"You'll be glad to know I've been in touch with

Colonel Primrose, Grace," Alice said, pouring me a cup of fragrant Island coffee. "He's coming out right away."

She looked over at her husband. "I must tell you, Harry," she said. It couldn't have been more lightly. "Grace has an idea that there's somebody locked in the air-raid shelter . . . a spy, or something."

Harry Cather, in the act of taking his paper up again, stopped short. The blank look of bewilderment on his face turned slowly into an amused and patient smile that in turn broke into an outright laugh. It wasn't unkind at all, just amused. I would have felt like a complete fool except that I was sharply aware of Mary's eyes fixed on me, not blank now but instantly horrified, uncomprehending and accusing at the same time . . . so that I felt not only a fool but a knave too.

"I've told her I thought she'd been around Colonel Primrose too long," Alice said. "But it's easy to make sure. I didn't want to disturb you, Harry. After all, if he's locked up he can't get out. That's certain."

Harry Cather smiled again. "I trust he hasn't drunk up my keg of okolehao. It's the last one I've got. Let me know when you catch him, girls."

He went back to his paper.

Aunt Norah said, *"Spies!"* and went back to her papaya.

Mary was trying to go on with hers. Her lids were down and burning along the edges at the roots of her dark amber lashes. Once I saw her give a quick side-ways glance from her mother to her aunt, but otherwise she kept her eyes down. Kumumato took my empty glass of pineapple juice and put half a solo papaya in front of me.

"We're expecting a colonel, Kumumato," Alice said. "Let me know as soon as he comes." She turned her head, listening. "Isn't that a car coming in? It's prob-ably him now."

She pushed back her chair and got up. She was half-way through the house to the door before the ring of the bell came like a remote and hollow peal of derisive laughter to my particular ears.

The rest of us got up too. Harry followed into the house. Mary still wasn't looking at me. As I glanced at her I saw her reach down and pick up, out of the chair she was sitting in, my evening bag. Kumumato went calmly on removing the dishes. Aunt Norah stood over by the rail, looking, I suppose, for termites. A termite hole or any other would have been an elegant place for me at just that point. I could already see, or hear, the pattern, polite and incredulous—"We must do everything possible to relieve your mind, my dear. Mainlanders see a spy behind every hibiscus bush"— that would make me look like a ridiculous idiot to my old friend Colonel Primrose, and of course to Ser-geant Buck who had that opinion already.

Because it really wasn't necessary to tell me more plainly that Roy Cather was no longer in the air-raid shelter.

14

THEY WERE COMING OUT NOW, AND THE
voice was the voice of John Primrose but the uniform
was the uniform of the Army. My jaw dropped. It
was the first time I'd ever seen him in uniform and
I hadn't known he was on active duty. His eagles were
bright and shiny new. I looked automatically two
paces behind him and there, of course, was Sergeant
Buck's great figure, in uniform too, though he'd never
really been out of it in spite of his external raiment.
He stood there rock-ribbed, ramrod-spined, lantern-
jawed and viscid-eyed, blood brother of the petrified
fish as he had always been.

"Good morning, Mrs. Latham."

Colonel Primrose came out on the lanai. His black
sparkling X-Ray eyes moved briefly around the group.
He shook my hand briefly.

"They tell me you tried to get in touch with me
last night."

My jaw had sunk first. Now it was my heart. Something had happened. Maybe it was the uniform, I don't
know. But there was no amused reassuring affection in
his face or none of the gentle amused regard I was

used to seeing in him in Washington, or wherever I'd called on him when anything alarming happened. It wasn't Colonel Primrose any more. It was the Army.

"Well, I did," I said. It's hard to explain how unsure I felt. It wasn't just being made to look ridiculous. It was being made to look hysterical and stupid, a female trouble maker in a war area that has no use for such.

"I'm afraid there's not much point in it," I added feebly.

Harry Cather relieved the strain momentarily— "This is my sister, Mrs. Bronson, and my daughter Mary"—before he turned to Kumumato. "Bring the key to the shelter, please. The one in the pantry if you're going down."

The house man gave a sort of ducking bow that made him suddenly like a servant again and made me curiously aware, even at such a moment, that usually he wasn't like one exactly.

Mary was standing straight and slim, her chin up, her cheeks flushed a little.

"Don't go, Kumumato," she said quietly. "I have the keys to the shelter."

I was convinced I was losing my mind then, if I hadn't already. And everybody stared at her, speechless—even her mother. There wasn't a flicker that I could see in any face to indicate which one was acting and which was legitimately as astounded as he looked. Colonel Primrose stood there silently.

Mary opened my bag and reached inside. I knew there wouldn't be any keys there. I was sure of that. And I was wrong. There were keys there. She brought them out, two of them, and put them down on the table. Harry Cather looked at them and at her, oddly.

"But . . . those aren't the shelter keys, Mary." He frowned a little. "Those are the keys to the front door. The shelter keys are square on top—these are round." He turned to the house man. "You'll find them in the usual places, I imagine. Go and get them, both of them, please."

Colonel Primrose was looking at Mary, and she was looking at the keys, the red spots in her cheeks fading a little before they suddenly got much brighter again. She looked up at Colonel Primrose.

"I'm sorry—I thought these were them," she said. She looked quickly over at me and back at them. "It's a curious mistake for me to make," she added calmly. "I don't see how I ever came to do it."

"Suppose we have a look at the shelter," Colonel Primrose said calmly.

We went down to it. Mary, walking with me, put her hand on my arm as we came up to the door. It was closed, but the spray of orchids that had been caught in it wasn't caught there any more. One spray hung down. The mangled one had been cut off.

"The door isn't locked, you see," Harry Cather said. He looked back at Mary. "You thought you'd locked it?"

"I must have made a mistake."

Harry Cather looked puzzled, but said nothing. He swung the door open and turned on a light at the panel by the door. Colonel Primrose stepped ahead of him.

"Just a minute, please," he said. "Buck."

He went in. Sergeant Buck, who had been bringing up the rear, did a double-quick forward. He's a very large man, and was not unlike the camel going through the needle's eye as he followed inside.

I waited, feeling indescribably. In a few minutes Colonel Primrose came back to the door.

"Would you like to come and look for yourselves?"

He was speaking to Mary and me, excluding the others, I supposed, as not needing to be shown.

Inside I could see why the young captain had said it was a honey. It was quite literally from soup to nuts —the soup in cans and the macadamia nuts in jars and tinned things in between in the large cupboard at the end of a quite spacious room. There was a small oil cookstove and two couches. Everything needed was there—everything except a shred of visible evidence that it had ever been used by Roy Cather or anybody else. Unless, I thought suddenly, the fact that it was spotless was visible evidence of a negative sort. I'm not much of a housekeeper, but I can tell when a room has recently been cleaned. Even the pillows on the couches were freshly fluffed up.

Colonel Primrose opened the door of a small washroom. It was empty—and clean. He lifted the woven cover on each sofa. Nobody was under either of them.

Nobody was in the radio cabinet, in the knife and fork drawer in the cupboard, or under the edge of the floor mat.

He looked at Mary and me.

"Are you satisfied, Mrs. Latham? And you, Miss Cather?"

Mary nodded. I said, "Quite. I'm sorry I bothered you."

I was aware of Sergeant Buck, stooping a little to keep his head from denting the concrete ceiling. His fish-gray eyes were fixed on me. It's the first time I can remember looking at him that his dead pan didn't turn slowly the brassy color of a tarnished sugar bucket before he looked away—and usually spat to one side as a critical comment that the Articles of War didn't allow him to express otherwise. I had a grim feeling that he was reviewing those Articles in his mind now, trying to think if they listed the offense of calling out the military on what he calls a wild moose chase as sufficient to indicate a blank wall at sunrise, and what the proper wording of the order to open fire was. And I know he was feeling he'd never have to worry about the altar as a bleak alternative again . . . if he ever had to.

"If anybody had been here, there'd be some sign of it?" Colonel Primrose asked patiently. "That's reasonable, isn't it, Mrs. Latham?"

"Oh, very," I said. I took hold of Mary's arm. "Come along, darling."

Sergeant Buck backed against the wall for us to pass.

Behind him—I hadn't noticed it when we came in—was a niche in the concrete wall. In it was a telephone. I caught my breath sharply, remembering the night before and Alice Cather's desperate cry before she staggered and fell forward in a dead faint in the passage . . . and the four telephone calls around dinner time just after Mary had locked the shelter . . . and Kumumato's bland assurance it was the wrong number.

For a split second I stopped. Colonel Primrose stopped behind me. I wanted to turn—but I didn't. I went on with Mary. If he wanted any help from us he could at least have asked what our side of the story was before he came to the conclusion that we were just a couple of hysterical females seeing things at night. It wasn't like him, really.

"Is everything all right, Grace?"

Alice, standing there with her husband and Aunt Norah, was so instantly sympathetic that I could see the doors of a padded cell at St. Elizabeth's closing on me.

I nodded. Just then I felt Mary's arm in mine tighten. She was looking along the bank where the orchids grew, toward the pool, not the house. Another spray down near the ground was broken off that we'd passed without seeing. There were others too, not broken but bruised. I turned and looked quickly up at the lanai where I'd spent the night. I was about two feet from the bank. I had to move another two feet away from it to see the chaise longue through the redwood railing. Even if it had been a brilliant moonlight night, I could never have seen Roy Cather creep away along the dark shadow of the bank, or any one. And Uncle Roy at least I'd never hear, not jungle-silent as I knew he could be.

Then it was my arm that tightened on Mary's. Coming around the bend in the coral road from the back way to the cottage was Swede. He was alone and not in a bathing suit but in uniform, and all properly so and looking curiously businesslike for some reason.

"Oh, Swede, how nice," Alice said. "This is Harry's sister, Mrs. Bronson, Lieutenant Ellicott. Oh, and Colonel Primrose."

Swede saluted smartly after speaking to Aunt Norah. Colonel Primrose came forward, his hand out.

"Hello, Swede," he said cordially. "I heard you were around. I was supposed to bring you some ciga-rettes from your father, but I gave them to a needy civilian en route. Be sure to thank him, won't you? You know the Sergeant."

Swede, who knew the Sergeant at least from the time he'd sent a baseball through Colonel Primrose's window on P Street when he was in school, winked as he returned a salute.

He turned to Alice. I thought there was something oddly intent about him.

"I guess this is your air-raid shelter, Mrs. Cather. Mind if I have a look at it?"

"Not at all," Alice said. If she was surprised nothing

indicated it. I don't know whether her added remark was malicious. "—Mrs. Latham will probably be glad to show it to you—she's interested in it too."

I said, "Surely." I didn't look at Colonel Primrose. The rest of them moved off toward the house, except Mary, who started slowly the other way, by herself, toward the pool.

Swede had to bend a little too as we went in, through the angled concrete slabs that kept the light from showing outside. He looked around silently for a minute. Then he said, "Neat."

"Very," I said. I added, "I thought you were leaving us."

"I was," he answered. "I decided to stay."

Something in his voice made me look at him intently.

"What's the matter?"

He sat down on the couch and looked up at me gravely.

"That's what I'd like to know, Grace. Sit down here and tell me, lady. Just what *is* going on around here?"

I sat down, but I shook my head.

"It seems I don't know. You'll have to ask Colonel Primrose."

"What's he here for?"

I didn't quite know what to say.

"Because Mary and I think we're Joan of Arc. We hear voices. We see things in the air."

He shot me a look that was as abrupt as his questions had been.

"Yeah? Did you see who was in here last night, by any chance?"

His light blue eyes were hard. And I was getting more and more puzzled momentarily.

"Nobody," I said. "That's official. Look around for yourself."

He did look around.

"Somebody was here, Grace," he said evenly. "And I'm going to find out who it was if it hurts somebody."

"What makes you think so?" I asked. "I mean, that there was somebody here?"

"A friend of mine told me so." He got up. "Is there a phone?"

I pointed over at the niche in the wall.

"Then it was straight dope." He said it more to himself than to me, as if he hadn't entirely believed it before that. "—This friend of mine got a call to come up here . . ."

I looked at him, understanding a little—or probably it would be better to say, thinking I understood a little.

"Friend named Corinne?" I asked.

The color came up from his tan shirt collar and stopped somewhere midway to his thick blond hair.

"It doesn't matter what the name is," he said curtly. "I want to know what's going on."

"Why not ask her?"

"She doesn't know anything more about it than I

do. She just got a call to come up here and get him out of this fancy dump."

"—And did she?" I asked.

"No. It was locked up tight as a bank vault."

"And she didn't tell you who he was?"

He shook his head.

"Why not?"

"She doesn't want to make trouble for the Cathers, so she wouldn't tell me his name. She told me something about him. He's a guy that's been sick quite a long time. He helped her father and mother, and the Cathers have done him out of quite a lot of money. He came to try to collect, and this is what happens to him."

He looked around the shelter again, and I looked at him, trying to figure out things myself.

"What is your interest in it, Swede?"

"I'm interested because Corinne asked me to keep an eye out for the old fellow," he said simply. "She doesn't seem to think he's very safe up here, among the mountain lions. If he's got money, or if he had it, she's probably got something. Our hostess seems to have an exaggerated idea of its importance. It wasn't till she discovered my aunt's money was going some place else that she decided I wasn't good enough for her charming daughter."

The sudden bitterness in his voice was disturbing. It would have been folly to try to tell him anything else just then.

"That was the way she wrecked Corinne's marriage to poor old Ben," he went on. He was speaking with a kind of determined brutality about him that wasn't like him, as I remembered, at all. "Ben was nuts about Mary too. He got over it out here and married Corinne . . . and right away our lady friend wrote him that Mary wasn't going to marry me after all. Ben wasn't himself, I guess—anyway, he blew his top and treated Corinne like a dog and went out and got himself a hunk of lead first crack out of the box. He wrote her he wouldn't come back. It was a tough deal for her, poor kid. Oh, well, what the hell . . . that's water under the bridge. But this deal doesn't look so good to me either, Grace. That's why I stayed up. I've got an old bone to pick with your friend Mrs. Cather, lady."

"Corinne must be a pretty fascinating girl," I said.

"She's had a rotten break from so-called white people," he said quietly. "There's some old guy here that was decent to her and her family when they were practically outcasts, I guess. Anything I can do to help her help him . . . okay."

"Okay, Sir Galahad," I said. I got up. "I think it's wonderful. Now if I were you, what I'd do is go up and tell Colonel Primrose all about it. Maybe if you'll tell him somebody was here, he'll believe you. He's cased the joint and he says nobody's been here. If Corinne knows better, why don't you get her to come and talk to him?"

Swede got up too.

"I always thought you were a friend of mine, Grace," he said quietly. "Can't you give me a break just once? Corïnne has to live here until the war's over. The Cathers are big shots. She'd have one hell of a time if anybody thought she was trying to pull a fast one on her betters. You can see that yourself, Grace. She hasn't got a chance. That's why she didn't speak to Mrs. Cather at once. You can see that."

I could certainly see something—through a glass darkly—and it was a very good guy who was ready to believe whatever Corinne Farrell told him because his pride was still raw and hurt. Mary's unexpected presence when he was trying to forget her, far from healing it at all, was salt being heavily rubbed in.

"You go talk to Colonel Primrose, then," I said. "He'll probably decide you're psychoneurasthenic too, and then you can stay in Honolulu."

"Thanks a lot," he said. "I'll do just that, right now."

15

OUT ON THE TERRACE, ASSUMING I WAS GOING to the house Swede started toward the pool, and changed his course abruptly. Mary was standing on the rim of the pool, her back to me. I must have come very quietly over the grass, because I was almost at her side before she was aware of me. She gave a violent start and turned. Her eyes were very wide, and she was as waxen white as the pale broken spray of butterfly orchids she'd picked and was holding in her hand.

It was too late for her to turn and run, though I thought that was the only too evident impulse written in every line of her body. She stood looking at me silent and so white-faced for a moment. Then she moistened her lips and put her hand out and touched my arm.

"Look, Grace," she whispered. "Down there. Don't say anything. Just look."

Her voice was so constricted it was hardly audible.

"Straight down. Be careful."

She held on to me. I leaned forward a little, past the edge of the pool there, and looked. The dark scum

on the face of the rock that marked the path of the
drain water from the pool was like a long green worm
writhing down, ending, where a tree growing out of a
cleft half-way to the bottom caught and held it, in
a pale-white blob. And it was only the grace of God
that kept me, even when she was holding on to me,
from hurtling down the rock to meet it.

It wasn't a white blob. It was a face. It was a human
face, rigid and white and terrible, staring up at us out
of the leaves of the tree coming out of the rock. It
was the face I'd seen in the trees beyond across the
ravine, but clean shaven now and all deadly white.
It was the face in the shadows on the lanai. And it
was again *just* a face. The body was invisible, still
camouflaged in the spotted jungle suit that mingled
with the leaves and branches holding it caught there,
suspended, half-way down to the tumbling stream at
the bottom of the narrow gorge. It was unbelievably
like the head of a thin monstrous snake slipping down
the face of the rock.

Mary was tugging at my arm, pulling me back.

"It's him," she whispered. "He's dead. They . . .
they've killed him. Come back. Don't look any more.
He's dead—he's dead."

We moved back onto the grass and sat down. My
knees were too weak to hold me up, and I guess hers
were too. Behind us was the empty shelter. The spray
of orchids in Mary's hand must have been broken, I
thought, as somebody dragged his body under the

shadow of the bank to the pool and around it, to the one path the overflow kept open, where his body would go down without leaving a telltale trail behind it. The tree that caught him and held him was Fate stepping in again. If he'd gone on into the bottom of the chasm, he might have been hidden forever.

Mary sat beside me silently, staring at the broken spray of orchids. Suddenly as if she were thinking what I was, she threw it away and stared at it, her eyes wider still. Then, just as abruptly, she got to her feet, went over to the bank and bent down. She lifted a small square of redwood set in the grass, and before I realized what she was doing, as she reached into the hole she'd uncovered I heard the slush of rushing water as the main vent of the pool opened. The water in it went down inch after inch, rapidly, leaving the blue painted surface an expanding empty border.

I looked at her open-mouthed.

From below, quite audible above the sound of the falling water, there was a soft crashing thud. Roy Cather's body had gone the rest of its grim journey.

"Mary!" I said again.

She waited quietly, still very white-faced, her eyes fixed steadily on the emptying pool. The last inch drew into a thin stream hurrying to the outlet and disappearing in silence before she bent down and closed the vent. I saw the water creeping in again, building itself up slowly. She put the redwood block back and came over to me.

"We didn't see anything, Grace," she said steadily. "There's nothing there now. That means there never was anything there. Same like the shelter."

I got up. I don't know whether it was that face at the end of the trail of green slime, or Mary's calm and deliberate turning of Colonel Primrose's argument against him so ruthlessly, or whether it was being in the position—and really, now—of accessory after the fact, that was the most disturbing. Maybe it was just all three together.

"You can't do that, Mary," I said weakly.

"I've done it. You can go tell Colonel Primrose if you want to. I won't try to stop you. He's dead. He can't hurt anything any more. That's what's really important. It doesn't matter who . . . who killed him. Or . . . maybe he just slipped. Maybe he was going for a swim and slipped over the side."

"In that case it would have been better to leave him where he was, wouldn't it?" I asked.

"—People don't go swimming with their clothes on," she said calmly. She stopped and put her hand to the bank to steady herself.

"It's horrible, it's simply horrible," she said. "But he can't do anything now. He shouldn't ever have come here. He should have stayed in Japan. He was a traitor, Grace—he deserved to die. But how ghastly!"

She turned, listening, her eyes widening again.

"Grace—they're coming! They're going to find him. Listen!"

I listened. I could hear the roar of planes, coming closer and closer. Then I saw them . . . two small silver ships coming over the top of the mountain range, banking down sharply to sweep along so close over our heads that we could almost reach up and touch them.

Mary's face as she looked at me was bewildered and as blank as a sheet of writing paper.

"Let's go in," she said quickly.

She looked back up at the two planes searching the mountainside.

"I . . . I've got to see my mother."

The garden was empty as we crossed over it to the house. Harry Cather was up on the lanai, still reading his paper. Aunt Norah was with him, but neither Alice Cather nor Colonel Primrose was in sight. Sergeant Buck had disappeared, so had Swede. Behind us was the pool quietly filling up to the brim again, and below it, deep in the dark gorge of rock and fern and trees growing out of the fissures in its rugged sides, was Roy Cather.

Mary didn't look back. Whatever the turmoil of doubt and suspicion and fear inside her, it wasn't visible . . . not until we'd gone up the steps from the game room into the hall and started out to go through the living room to the lanai. Then she did falter. She stopped just before we got to the two steps leading down into the living room.

Her aunt's voice, high-pitched and harsh and curiously nagging, came through to us.

". . . all I asked was what he's talking to Alice so long about," she was saying. "Why isn't it you he's talking to, Harry? I should think he'd talk to a man, not a woman, if he wants information. It's very inconsiderate, I think."

A sudden pain drained all the blue out of Mary Cather's eyes. There were white lines around her lips that the scarlet red of her lipstick only made a sharper white.

"You'll have to do what you think right, Grace," she said. "—Let's wait till she shuts up."

—If ever, I thought. The voice kept up an incessant flow. It stopped then, but only for a moment.

"Harry," it said then. "Who is this Ellicott boy? I've heard that name before."

Mary closed her eyes and leaned her head against the door frame.

"Oh, dear," she said. "Now it's coming. I knew she'd remember it was him I was engaged to. I don't think I can stand any more."

It was coming, but it was not what either of us would ever have guessed.

"Ellicott, Ellicott," Aunt Norah said. "I know, Harry. Put down your paper and listen. It was last night at dinner some one brought his name up. In connection with that girl you sent to school. Corinne. You remember her, Harry. Well . . ."

Mary had opened her eyes and raised her head abruptly, her body then quite motionless.

"They applied for a marriage license yesterday,

Corinne and this boy Ellicott. His commanding officer couldn't do anything about it . . . or wouldn't, for some reason or other. It seems———"

The girl standing by me moved then, and it must have taken all the strength she had left. And I couldn't do a thing. She went over to the door, not very steadily. Her face was as pale as ashes.

"I'm going to my room," she said. "Do what you want to about———"

That was all she got out. She was gone then, out of the front door so she wouldn't be seen by her father and her aunt.

I stood looking after her. She seemed so fragile and vulnerable, her head bent forward a little, moving across the sundrenched driveway, that when she stopped abruptly I started to go out to her. But I stopped too. She'd turned her head and was standing stock-still, looking across the road. She was looking at Swede. He'd stopped too, on his way to the cottage or back to the house to see Colonel Primrose, I couldn't tell. He was looking across at her. I don't know what impulse it was that moved him, but he took an abrupt step forward to cross over to her.

And he stopped again. She was running down into the gully, the back way to her room. Swede stood there looking after her a long time before he turned and cut off slowly down into the lane that led through the trees to the cottage. I saw him stop again and stand there looking up at the planes, still sweeping low over the mountainside. He was still standing there watching them when I turned and went through the passage to my own room and closed the door.

I didn't see Colonel Primrose before he left. I heard him leave Alice Cather's sitting room, and maybe what I felt was a sharp twinge of good old-fashioned jealousy. Or maybe it was just pique, a childish annoyance that he hadn't felt it important to bother about consulting me. Whatever it was, I heard him leave her sitting room, and her voice, as light and confident as ever, assuring him that mistakes were bound to happen and it was really quite all right, she understood perfectly. After a little I heard a car leave the driveway.

I lay down and closed my eyes. I was tired, among other things, but I was only pretending I was asleep when Alice opened my door and looked in. She closed it quietly and tip-toed down the passage to her room, and then I did go to sleep. It was almost lunch time when I woke. Outside Tommy and Dave were making a terrific racket coming out of the pool, but as I listened the rest of the house seemed preternaturally quiet. It may have been the lull before the storm about to break.

I changed my dress and went out by way of the passage. I intended to find Mary and say whatever I could to her, which certainly was not very much.

"Grace—is that you, dear? Do come in."

Alice called me through her open door. She was in her bedroom. I waited in the sitting room.

"I'll be ready in just a moment. The boys are coming down for lunch. I'm so sorry you were upset about all this. Colonel Primrose is charming really, isn't he?"

I didn't think so, at the moment, but I let it pass.

"He left a message for you, dear. He's going to send a car this evening. He wants you to have dinner with him somewhere."

I said, "Oh, really?" What I thought was just a plain quiet "Nuts," which is the vernacular effect my sons have had on my speech in the course of years.

I'd wandered over to the lanai waiting for her to come out.

"I wonder where Mary's got to?" she said through the door. "I haven't seen her since morning."

I turned back, thinking I'd better tell her where Mary had got to, but I didn't get that far. I stared up at the portrait of Roy Cather over the mantelpiece. At least I stared at where the portrait of Roy Cather had been. It was gone. In its place was a portrait of a Chinese vase with a single stalk of shell ginger in it. It was a very nice picture, but it wasn't Roy Cather. I looked away quickly as Alice came out.

She was smiling and superbly at ease. She put her arm affectionately through mine.

"You must have thought I was very wicked yesterday," she said. "Putting poor old Norah out of the house the way I did. She really means well, and she's had a wretched life, over on that ranch. Works like a horse. I oughtn't to begrudge her a little pleasure here. After all, the place really is half hers."

It had been a third hers the morning before. I wondered if I knew what Alice meant. And I think I did, perhaps, and she did mean what I thought, until just a very little later.

We were all in the living room having a cocktail, with a buffet lunch waiting out on the lanai. And we were all there. Whether Harry Cather had told Aunt Norah to pipe down about Swede's marriage license I don't of course know, but she was talking to Tommy and Dave about horses, and they didn't look as if they'd heard the other yet. Swede was there, to my surprise, unless he figured being there was closer to the trail he was apparently bent on following by himself, without Colonel Primrose's help. From a distance in the cool shaded room Mary looked lovely, finely drawn but self-controlled and self-contained. She wasn't looking at Swede or Swede at her.

Outside the planes were still flying very low.

"—Are we all here?" Alice Cather said, smiling around the room.

I shall never forget that line. It was a cue for the little gods waiting, prompting, in the wings. It couldn't have been neater if it had been written in the original book. The front door opened. There was no knocking, and no bell ringing. Just the door opening.

We turned as one man and looked.

Corinne Farrell walked in. She walked in smiling, white teeth, black hair, red lips, dark shining eyes, slim and lithe and quite unabashed, the situation hers and completely in control. She came to the archway and stopped at the top of the two steps. She looked around at the frozen dumfounded faces staring blankly back at her.

"Where shall they put my bags, Aunt Alice?" she inquired. "I have come to stay. My father tells me the house is ours too. One-third ours. I think so."

She looked around the long silvery cool room.

"It is very nice. I think we will change the sofas. Otherwise it is very nice. I think I will like it here. Yes, I think so."

She looked back at Alice Cather.

"Where shall they put my bags did you say, Aunt Alice?"

16

"WHERE DO THEY PUT MY BAGS, AUNT ALICE?"
Corinne repeated it again, still standing, bland and
smiling, at the top of the steps that came down into
the living room.

I wondered, as I've wondered many times since,
what she really felt like just then . . . whether inside
she was as blandly confident as she looked . . . whether
in announcing her legal right to a share in the house
near the Pali she had any sudden curdling emotion of
fear. I would have had it. I would have taken one look
at the faces in that room and I would have run like a
rabbit. She didn't understand, I suppose, that occidentals
when put to it can be as impassively oriental as the
best oriental of them all. Perhaps it was because nobody
turned so much as a hair of the varied assortment of
yellow, gray, gold, black, red and white hair in the
room that she didn't see there was dynamite, and how
intensely hot the fuse was. But the silence and the
total lack of expression that so instantly blotted out
the dumfounded amazement everybody felt seeing
her walk in should have been enough to warn her.

I don't know how to describe the overall picture. It was like nothing I'd ever seen before. Whatever the emotions—and highly varied they must have been, with Swede Ellicott, his application to marry the gal in his pocket, at one pole and Alice Cather at the other, and all the rest of them in between, including Dave Boyer who'd threatened to kill her before she married Swede—there was no evidence of them on a single face turned toward her. And the Cathers were superb. That in particular is why, if I'd been Corinne, I'd have been afraid, suddenly very much afraid, and I'd have left then and there.

But she didn't. She waited, smiling and confident, looking at Alice, waiting for her to tell her where to put her bags.

"You will have to discuss that with Mr. Cather, Mrs. Farrell," Alice said calmly.

Harry went across the room toward the girl.

"I'm afraid we have no room at the moment, Corinne."

She glanced at him briefly and looked back at Alice Cather.

"I think you can find room, Aunt Alice. I think so."

The veiling of the threat was gossamer soft and quite thick, and if I hadn't known about Uncle Roy I wouldn't have recognized it.

Mary, who had been very still, her face expressionless, standing there where Mrs. Bronson had been talking about horses, stepped forward.

"If Mrs. Farrell has a legal right to stay here, Dad, I'm sure she's welcome. She can have my room. I'll move in with Grace."

She turned to her mother inquiringly. As Alice was silent for a moment it occurred to me that her self-control had had a lot of strain on it the last few days. But it stayed intact under a powerful surface tension, and even under the blow that came next, a bomb from the blue.

"You see, Mother," Mary said quietly. "Mrs. Farrell and Swede are going to be married. They won't have a great deal of time before he goes back forward. She probably wants to be here where he is as much as possible. I understand they applied for a license yesterday."

The momentary silence was so thick it could have been cut with a very dull knife. When Tommy Dawson cut it the knife was not dull.

"—And that," he said, "sure puts our hero in a lousy spot."

I don't suppose there could have been a more accurate statement of what must have been in everybody's mind. Swede's jaw hardened. He looked over at Tommy, and then suddenly and quite unexpectedly there was a flicker of light in his eyes.

"—Right," he said.

He started across the room and stopped in front of Mary. "Sorry," he said. It was clipped off very short. He went on to Alice and Harry Cather. "I'm

very sorry, Mrs. Cather . . . good-bye, sir, and thank
you." He went up the two steps to Corinne's side.

"We're off," he said shortly. "Where are your bags?"
She stood motionless.

"I'm not going. I'm staying. This house belongs to
my father too. I have as much right here as they have.
They can't make me go."

"Okay, lady," he said evenly. "Stay ahead. I'm getting out."

He started on.

"No, Swede! You stay, as my guest . . ."

A flush dyed his cheeks a dull angry red. I'd thought
maybe Corinne was a really bright girl up to that point.

"Hardly," he said. "And you'd better come with
me."

"I am staying. You may go if you like."

He started on just as Alice Cather spoke.

"Swede . . . we hope you will stay."

She went over toward the steps, Corinne's dark eyes
moving with her.

"Corinne has a right to be here. If she wants to use
it, she can. Under the circumstances we'd prefer you'd
stay too. We'd be much happier if you would."

"I agree, Ellicott," Harry Cather said quietly. "It'll
be much simpler for everybody."

I suppose as Swede stood there what was going
through his mind was that maybe it was simpler, for
everybody but him. And he did a rather surprising
thing. He looked steadily over at Mary. And Corinne

Farrell was bright enough, or female enough, to be aware of it instantly, even without looking at him. Her dark glance flashed from Alice for the first time and rested on her daughter. There was no nonsense about oriental impassiveness there just then. It was a quick passionate hatred, burning with fire and brimstone, so revealing it was shocking.

"I think you'd better stay," Mary said. She turned to her mother. "Let's have lunch. I'll move my things out as soon as we're through."

And then, in this incredible or at least to me utterly bewildering scene of cross currents and purposes and motives, so incomprehensible to my mind that I didn't know why any one of them was acting as he was with the possible exception of Corinne, Aunt Norah came suddenly to articulate life. She was staring across at the half-Japanese girl, what I may call her termite expression at the highest pitch I'd seen it get to.

"—Just a minute, Alice. Am I to understand that this young woman is Roy Cather's daughter?"

Harry Cather answered. He looked years older, and tired. "I'm afraid you are, Norah."

"Why have I never been told?"

He shook his head. "Just easier not to," he said patiently.

"It was easier to pay her school bills and——"

"Much easier. Roy . . . wasn't here."

Mrs. Bronson's eyes blazed. "That . . . *scoundrel!*"

Alice Cather was across the room in a flash, her

hand on her sister-in-law's arm. *"Please,* Norah!"

But Corinne came coolly down into the room. "And my mother," she said. She looked around her. "To think that my mother was once a servant in this house. It is democracy. It couldn't happen anywhere but in America . . ."

"—Success story . . ." Tommy Dawson said. It was aside and sotto voce, but not enough so.

"Not exactly," Harry Cather said. "We might as well get the record straight. Her mother came from a good family. My father had business dealings with their firm. They wanted their daughter to learn American housekeeping methods—she was supposed to marry into the consular service and be sent to the United States. My mother agreed to take her. She was an apprentice rather than a servant. She was only here a year."

Corinne looked up at him starry-eyed. "And that was when my father married her?"

"I'm afraid not," he said quietly. "She happened to have married already—without my parents' knowledge. She learned American ways quickly. The divorce from that marriage went through after she left."

"But she left with my father?"

"I'm afraid she did. We've never been proud of it, Corinne."

"But I am," she said quickly. "I am proud that he stayed——"

"I think it's a subject we can dispense with, Mrs.

Farrell," Alice Cather said quietly. "It's time for lunch. We can talk about this later." She motioned to Kumumato, who'd stood, impassive throughout, by the door to the service steps.

I wouldn't say that that lunch was a gay or lively party, or even surface-smooth. We got our food and sat in various places. I took one look at Dave Boyer and looked quickly away. He was the way he'd been at the hotel Sunday afternoon, his face dark. Tommy Dawson, hovering as near Mary as he could, was far from himself. Kumumato dropped the rolls he was bringing in, gathered them up hastily, took them out and brought in others, or maybe the same ones dusted off. Swede Ellicott sat or moved about in a large silent orbit of his own . . . with Corinne a worshipful satellite. I saw where those girls got their charm. When he took out a cigarette she was there with a lighted match, and when he sat down after he'd got his food she pulled a stool over and sat demurely at his feet, smiling and serene.

Alice Cather was controlled still, but with a much greater and more apparent effort. It came to me with a little shock, looking at her once, that the matter with her was that she was simply frightened. Her voice was still liquid, but it was liquid flowing thinly over jagged rocks. Whether she'd been frightened all day, or whether Corinne's abrupt arrival had brought some new menace she hadn't counted on and was just now realizing, I didn't dare to guess.

Mary was very pale, and once when our eyes met I saw fear in hers too, fear and an appeal so poignant that it was more disturbing than the fear.

And the smile stayed on Corinne's red lips.

Alice got up at last.

"If you'll come with me, Mrs. Farrell, we'll get this straightened out," she said steadily. "Grace . . . will you take the boys down to the game room? There's a cupboard with a backgammon board, and——"

"Surely," I said. I was afraid for a dreadful instant that I was going to have to show them the garden . . . like the young captain who was ordered to take me out at an awkward moment.

17

"I'LL SEE ABOUT MY THINGS NOW," MARY SAID. She was gone at once along the lanai toward her room. Harry Cather and Aunt Norah had joined the family pow-wow, Tommy and Dave came with me. Swede stayed where he was, getting used, I supposed, to the strange sort of middle world on either side of which he had been cut out and cut in.

"Jeepers," Tommy said.

We sat down on the big sofa in front of the fireplace, not interested in the cupboard with the backgammon board and whatnot in it.

"*Jeepers!*"

He shook his red head back and forth.

"—Ain't stardust the perishable stuff. *Baby!* You know it's funny, but I almost felt sorry for that dame. She's so god-awful on the wrong course and hasn't brains enough to see it."

Dave Boyer scowled.

"She's got it figured all wrong," Tommy said. "She figures he hates the Cathers' guts. He'll be tickled to death to see 'em get a kick in their gold-plated teeth.

She'll show 'em up in a big way and they'll kick and
scream. But they don't. Mary comes through like an
angel. And then, my God, that handmaiden stuff! Did
you see her try to light his cigarette? Some fall for it,
lady—home, they're not so used to it. But it's like fly-
paper, you don't want to get your feet tangled up in
it in public."

He laughed mirthlessly. "The poor old Swede. Did
you pipe the blinders falling off? It's damn lucky you
have to wait three days from the time you put your
head in the noose till they spring the trap."

He put his hand out and shook Dave's shoulder.

"See, David? My old Pappy used to say, there's
more ways of killing a horse than choking it to death
with butter. All we had to do was wait for the Divine
Wind . . . Kamikaze on the home front."

"I wonder," Dave said laconically.

"He's through, David. He's got the old peepers
wide, starin' open, boy."

"Yeah. *She's* not through."

"—The Voice of Doom, eh. That's easy, David."

We heard the upstairs door open and Mary's voice.
". . . down with the rest of them," she was saying.
"Corinne will be along in a minute."

There were heavy steps behind hers, and she and
Swede came in.

"Hi, there. We're all set, you'll be happy to know.
My stuff's stowed in with yours, Grace. Move over,
children. We can't swim yet. What about a game of
gin?"

"Hearts," Tommy said. "I want to play hearts. On the floor."

"Michigan," Mary said.

"Michigan it is."

I sat there on the mat on the floor playing a card game, knowing that the body of a murdered man was in the ravine not a good stone's throw from where we sat, and that upstairs his daughter was wreaking a strange vengeance on . . . I almost thought, "his murderers," but backed away from it quickly. It was a statement I'd been avoiding making even to myself, because in effect I was saying Alice Cather had murdered him . . . or executed him was perhaps a better term. I felt bitterly sorry for her, wondering whether Corinne had already told Harry Cather what Alice had been so desperately trying to keep him from knowing. I looked at Mary. How she could be keeping her mind on the cards was more than I could see. The chips, though, were piling up in front of her.

Swede sat across from her between me and Dave, his pipe in the corner of his mouth, intent on his cards. Whatever was going on inside of him wasn't shown.

Tommy Dawson pushed his last chip into the center.

"Cleaned out," he said. "Unlucky at cards."

He took the hand Mary dealt him without looking at it, his eyes resting on her.

"Mary," he said, "—will you do me a favor?"

"If I can."

"You're the only one that can," Tommy said. "And

it's this. I'm nuts about you. I think you're wonderful. Will you marry me?"

I was the only one who looked at him. Swede and Dave Boyer were concentrating on sorting their cards.

"Well," Mary said, "I don't know, Tommy. It's very sudden, isn't it?"

"Not sudden at all."

He looked at his cards.

"Not at all sudden. It's what's called a simple reiteration of a request brought to your attention in ours of the I don't know which instant . . . but in Washington, a long time ago. You were too young, then, lady. You didn't realize the stupendous opportunity——"

"It's sweet of you to give me another chance, darling," Mary said. She smiled across at him. "Perhaps I ought to——"

Swede put his cards down and got up.

"Excuse me, will you?"

He strode out onto the terrace and disappeared at the side of the garden toward the ravine.

"You dumb dope," Dave Boyer said angrily. "What the hell——"

"I have a right to propose to the young girl," Tommy said calmly. "I love her."

"You red-headed ape, she doesn't love you. It's your play."

Tommy tossed a card in.

"That's straight, Mary. No kidding. I mean it— every word of it."

Her cheeks were warm and her eyes suddenly a little too bright and liquid. "Thanks, Tommy," she said.

Alice Cather's voice coming down the stairway interrupted Dave Boyer's annoyed remark. "Mary? Grace?"

Mary put down her cards and got up. "Yes, Mother."

"Just down there, Mrs. Farrell," Alice was saying. "You'll find Swede and the other boys. They'll show you the garden——"

Tommy rose to his feet in a single motion. "Come on, David. We've got to see a dog.—So long, girls."

We waited at the bottom of the stairs for Corinne to come down. There was no doubt who'd been the victor. Her whole manner showed it.

"—Where are they going?" she asked, looking instantly after the boys.

"I don't know," Mary said. "Swede's outside, somewhere. Will you excuse me?"

I followed her toward the stairs. Corinne stepped past us toward the terrace entrance. Kumumato had come out of the service quarters door and was picking up the cards and chips we'd left on the floor. Corinne looked at him rather oddly for a moment, and then said something to him that I couldn't understand. And Mary, ahead of me, stopped short and half turned. The look on her face was extraordinary, almost as it had been at the pool after she'd seen Roy Cather's dreadful face staring up from the leafy shelf of the tree growing out of the cleft in the rocky wall.

She went on up. Corinne had gone out on the terrace. I looked at the houseman. He was still on one knee picking up the chips, but his hand rested motionless. He was looking after Corinne's disappearing figure, and I thought he was grinning.

"What did she say to him?" I asked after we'd closed the door.

Mary shook her head. "I only understand a little Japanese," she said. I thought she seemed both frightened, a little, and puzzled.

She didn't say any more until we were out on the lanai. Below us, sitting on the edge of the pool, were Swede and his prospective bride. She was speaking, her small kitten-soft hands fluttering like butterflies as she talked. Swede was listening, I suppose. He didn't look very happy, but I couldn't, off-hand, have thought of any reason why he should.

Mary looked over at them and turned away at once. "Let's go to our room," she said. "And look, Grace —don't leave me. I mean don't go back down town to stay. I couldn't stick this by myself."

She glanced back along the lanai.

"I don't understand it. Do you think she knows her . . . her father was here? She must, or she couldn't have come up this way."

I nodded. "I think she does."

"I don't want to think about any of it," she said slowly. "You see, either Mother knows he's dead, and doesn't dare put her out, or . . . she doesn't know, and thinks she has a right to be here. Because, you

see, the minute he's dead she has no more right. It's
the way I told you. It's only for their lifetime—Dad's
and Aunt Norah's and . . . his."

Her things were arranged on another dressing table
they'd put in the room, her clothes were hanging in
the closet with mine. She sat on her bed. We didn't
say anything. There was woefully little to say, that I
could think of.

Then from outside came a sudden silvery peal of
laughter . . . silvery, but not very mirthful. It was
much closer than the pool, in fact just outside under
the lanai.

"—I do not release you, Swede. You made a big
mistake. I think so."

"Okay. If that's how you feel, I'm stuck. But you're
getting out of here, and right now."

"Oh, no. I am staying. Aunt Alice wants me to stay."

"The hell she does."

"The hell she *does*," the girl repeated. "I think so.
Very anxious for me to stay . . . very anxious. And
I'll tell you why, Swede."

Mary sat there, rigid and intent.

"—I tell you why tonight, Swede—after I see—what
is it Tommy says—a dog. I'll tell you why."

The silvery peal of laughter came again. It was not
amused but cruel, and it had an almost hysterical break
in it.

"Stop it!"

It sounded as if he had taken her by the shoulder
and shaken her.

"If you've got anything to tell me, tell it now."

"Oh, very well. I will tell you right now. Come on. I'll tell your friends Tommy and David too. I'll tell that Mrs. Latham. We'll find them. You'll see what fine Americans . . ."

They were out of range, going past the house and up to the cottage. Mary sat perfectly still. She looked at me after a moment, but before she could speak we heard a light step on the lanai. It was Alice.

"Hello, dears," she said. "Exhausted? I don't blame you."

She dropped into a chair and looked out at the fluffy white clouds moving across the lovely clear blue of the sky under the low drooping roof of the lanai.

"Oh, dear," she said. "It's very difficult, isn't it?"

"—Did you hear Corinne just then, Mother?"

Alice turned slowly and looked at her. "Yes, dear. I don't see how any one in the house could help hearing her. Do you?"

"Then what is she telling Swede and the others? We've got a right to know too, Mother. What is she doing here? Why did she come? Why do you let her stay?"

Alice Cather was silent for a moment. When she spoke her voice was as liquid smooth and casual as ever.

"We've let her stay because she has a legal right to do so, Mary. I imagine she came for fairly obvious reasons."

She turned toward me, and her eyes met mine

directly, for an instant, for the only time, recently, that I could remember.

"And I imagine she is going to tell Swede that we have harbored a dangerous . . . spy in our house—even if the spy did happen to be her father. I don't know how she plans to get around that aspect of it."

She hesitated then, and went on quietly.

"It's true, of course—as you've both realized. Roy Cather was here. In the air-raid shelter. I tried to get rid of him before he could do any harm to anybody."

The silence in the little room prolonged. When Mary spoke next she didn't look at me.

"—Where is he now?"

"He's gone, back to Japan. Unless they catch him trying to get away."

I suppose I stared at her as Mary did.

"What do you mean, Mother?"

"Just that. He was leaving last night. That's why I was so appalled when I learned you two had locked the shelter so he couldn't get out. He found the scheme he had wouldn't work, and like a lot of other . . . cowards, he'd rather face death away from home."

"And you let him go?"

"I let him go. For many reasons."

There was another silence in which Mary looked at me and quickly away.

"Is it true, Mother . . ." She hesitated. "Is it true you . . . you're in love with him?"

"No, it is not." Her voice was clear and definite.

"It's not true at all. I used to be, once. Love can die as suddenly as any other human thing. You saw it happen this afternoon. It happened to mine for Roy Cather . . . many years ago. There are times when honor is more important than love."

"Then why did you let him go?"

"I wanted him away before Harry saw him, for one thing," Alice Cather said. "Or before he saw Harry. I wanted him to go back to his Japanese. He is a traitor to this country. He serves them. I wanted him to see what he'd get for selling them his soul. I wanted him to die there. I wanted to get him away from here before we were branded as traitors too. We'd never clear ourselves—no matter what proof we offered. He came to do a specific . . . job. He didn't do it. And he's gone."

"Is that what Corinne is going to tell the boys?"

"I assume it is."

There was a sound of voices outside, and Alice turned and went out. She stood looking down into the garden.

"What is it, Kumumato?"

A man's voice, not Kumumato's, answered. "We'd like to look at the air-raid shelter, ma'am. Is it all right?"

Alice nodded without speaking. She stood very still for an instant, her hand on the rail. Then she turned and went around the corner of the lanai.

Mary looked at me. "How much of that do you believe?"

"I don't know," I said.

"Frankly, I don't believe a damned word of it. And I wonder how much she believes."

I shook my head. "I've no idea, Mary."

She went out onto the lanai and looked over. "What are they doing, Kumumato?" she asked. In a moment she said, "Thanks," and came back in.

"Fingerprints, in the shelter," she said.

She sat down abruptly. "They must have found him," she said, after what seemed to me a long time. "Well, that means Corinne will go and the gendarmes will come. Aren't you glad you're a friend of ours? I should have told Tommy I wouldn't marry him . . . to save him the embarrassment of having to take it back when I fool him and say yes."

18

A LOW PRESSURE AREA HUNG HEAVILY OVER
the wide eaves of the house in the hills that afternoon,
in every sense of the word. The clouds, descending,
suddenly opened up and it rained. It really rained.
It poured. Below us, through an occasional break in
the swirling soot-colored banners of mist, Honolulu
lay clear and brilliant, the white garish jade she is.
Inside the house it was dry, but no more could be said
for it.

"I don't care if it is raining," Mary said. "I'm going
for a swim. I've got to get out of this house." And
she went.

In the living room Alice Cather and Aunt Norah
sat like two of the Three Grim Sisters. The only sound,
as I came in, was the sharp brittle click of Aunt Norah's
knitting needles, each click, I thought, in effect taking
off another small piece of Corinne Farrell's hide. Alice
had aged a thousand years.

"—How Harry can sit in there adding up figures
at a time like this is beyond me," Aunt Norah said.
Her needles clicked a wicked obbligato.

"It's better to be unconcerned," Alice said wearily.

"—I'm not unconcerned," Harry Cather said. He'd come up the passage to the room. "I simply see no way we can get the girl out of here, if she's determined to stay, except by time and patience."

The front door burst open at exactly that moment, and Corinne burst in. She'd been running. She was drenched to the skin. I couldn't tell whether it was rain water or tears pouring down her face. If tears they were tears of fury, because she slammed the door behind her and ran like something blind and wild past Harry Cather. Then the door of her room slammed.

"*Well*," said Aunt Norah.

"Let's skip it," Alice said. She went over to Harry. "Come on, darling, go back to your work."

She seemed determined still, I thought, to keep him wrapped in a rosy-pink cotton wool of ignorance of the drama being played out under his very nose, though how she could expect the whole Roy Cather epic, to continue on without his ever being aware of it was inconceivable to me.

She suddenly glanced over at the lanai, frowning a little, and went quickly across.

"What is it?" Norah Bronson demanded.

"Just Kumumato, taking Corinne some tea."

The needles clicked viciously.

"You're a fool to trust that man."

"Now, Norah," Harry said patiently.

"All right, Harry. Nobody will listen to me."

Alice shrugged and went over to her husband. "Come along, Harry."

"—I don't care if he's been around here a hundred and fifty *thousand* years," Mrs. Bronson said when they'd gone, to me or to the room generally. "I wouldn't trust one of them as far as I could see him in the dark. *They* don't know what that man was doing all the years before he came back to them because he couldn't get a job anywhere else."

She turned to me. "Why don't you sit down? Why are you standing there? You make me nervous."

I didn't sit down. She made me nervous too. I went past her out on the lanai and looked down at the pool. Mary was still there, and Tommy and Dave were standing there on the grass in swimming trunks, their faces turned up to the pelting rain.

"You people are crazy," I called.

They looked up at me. "Sure, why not," Tommy said cheerfully. "Everybody's gone nuts."

I turned back wondering where Swede was. Whatever Corinne had said at the cottage obviously hadn't made any difference to the two others.

Kumumato was just opening the door to go downstairs, the way Mary and I had gone from her room to avoid meeting her mother the day before. It seemed to me it had taken him a considerable time to serve a tea tray. Almost immediately after he closed the door, Alice came along behind him. She stopped at the door, started to open it and changed her mind. She was still frowning a little as she came on into the living room. Norah looked up at her. What it was they said to each other in the brief glance they exchanged I didn't know, but it was something. Aunt Norah began knitting more violently than ever.

That was the way things still stood, except that Mary and Tommy and Dave had come in and were playing the radio downstairs, when the doorbell rang a few minutes before five o'clock.

Alice closed her eyes for an instant as if expecting some new kind of doom to enter. She got up and went quickly across the room to open it herself, beating Kumumato, coming up from below stairs, by a quarter length.

There was a short silence before I heard her say, "Oh, yes, of course." She came back. "Grace, it's the car for you."

I looked up blankly from the paper I was reading.

"The car, from Colonel Primrose," she said.

I started over to the door. Everybody else was a little odd, to say the least, and maybe it was contagious.

"I've decided not to go," I said. "Tell the driver . . ."

I didn't go on. I'd made a mistake, and I realized it instantly. In the door was the massive khaki-colored pillar of granite, my old friend Sergeant Buck.

"Colonel's orders, ma'am," he said, menacingly, from the corner fissure of his lantern jaw.

It occurred to me that I was not in the Army and

that Colonel Primrose had no right to give me orders. It was a mistake, however, for me even to think so. Sergeant Buck's iron face congealed degrees of hard and cold.

"I . . . think you'd better go, dear," Alice said hastily.

"Colonel's orders," Sergeant Buck said. "Got to carry 'em out, irregardless."

For an absurd moment I determined not to be pushed around any longer. Was I a civilian and a taxpayer? Was I a mouse or was I a woman? I imagine, both, because as Sergeant Buck turned and spat out into the rain sluicing out of the gutter at the angle of the roof I was aware that he was, in effect, rolling up his sleeves, preparing himself for a particularly painful duty come hell or high water.

I went, quietly. There wasn't, obviously, anything else to do unless I wanted to get picked up bodily and hurled into the back of the car. Sergeant Buck did a double-quick around the car and got in under the wheel.

"—No offense meant, ma'am," he said.

It was the only time in our long association of mutual animosity and mistrust that I've failed to reply, "—And none taken, Sergeant." But I was mad, boiling mad, and I kept a silence as stony as the square, rigid back in front of me.

And being a woman, I got progressively more instead of less mad as we drove down and out past Fort Shafter into Kamehameha Boulevard, the wide highway cut through cane fields and rock to form a stupendous artery for the mighty fortress built up from the destruction of the morning of the Seventh. It's unlike any other highway in the world—a maelstrom of traffic, ammunition trucks, oil trucks, bulldozers, road machines, supply trucks, buses, jeeps and shiny new cars with stars on the plate in front . . . and beside it, carrying defense workers, tooting and rattling and strangely anachronistic, the Oahu Railroad, as absurd as a bamboo whistle in a magnificent orchestration of coordinated speed and power.

Ahead of us to the left high up in the green hills, the sun shone on the terraced roofs of the Navy's great Aiea Hospital. Below it where the bulldozers were cutting out the Red Hill road, hidden behind the low hills, lie the Pearl Harbor dead. Some three thousand of them lie there, under rows of small white crosses with the flag flying bravely above . . . the rock quarry behind them, the bulldozers in front and all around, grinding out a monstrous never-ceasing requiem. Their monument stretches out into the sea lanes and the air lanes from that reservoir of power, concentrated where three short years ago there were smoke and twisted steel, destruction and death.

We crossed the railroad tracks below Pearl Harbor and went into Hickam Field. There were planes on the runways and planes in the air, fighters, bombers, transports, hospital ships unloading evacués on stretchers into waiting ambulances. We could see them as we passed the great central terminal and went right toward the quarters, against the background of a carrier moving slowly out of Pearl Harbor, and the massive superstructures of fighting ships lying to.

Sergeant Buck stopped in front of a small mustard-colored bungalow with a red roof, a white oleander bush on one side of the steps and a pink one on the other. He conducted me in congealed silence into a small living room. There were stairs going up to the second floor. I waited for Colonel Primrose to come down them, a piece of my mind already cut out and sizzling hot to give him, but he didn't come. He wasn't even at home. I sat there, going over in my mind all past indignities I'd suffered at the hands of Colonel Primrose and his iron "functotum." It was unfortunate that when he came at last Sergeant Buck, standing guard on the front stoop, got to him first.

"—Some trouble, sir," I heard. He jerked his head in toward me. "—Want to clarify my skirts, sir."

Colonel Primrose when he came in did not seem impressed. He looked at me without a word of condolence or apology.

"They found the body," he said. "You will undoubtedly be happy to hear."

He put his cap on the radio.

I suppose it was a measure of the kind of existence I'd been living in for the last few days that I started to say, "What body?" But I stopped in time and said nothing, or rather, "Oh."

He stood there looking at me, almost grim and by no means friendly.

"Do you know, Mrs. Latham," he said deliberately, "that—I regret to say—I have you to thank for the most complete fiasco of my military career?"

That was a little more than I was prepared to take just then.

"I'm sorry," I said. "I don't know exactly what you're talking about. But you didn't give me a chance to tell you. You acted as if I was a complete fool. I could have told you there was a man in the shelter . . ."

Colonel Primrose drew and exhaled a very long breath, and when he spoke he sounded like a man who was counting up to twenty before picking up a blunt instrument.

"Listen, my dear lady," he said. "Some day, some time, maybe you'll learn to keep your pretty head out of other people's business and not to jump to conclusions. Listen to me. When I came out on the lanai at breakfast, one look at your face, and Mrs. Cather's face, and Mary Cather's face, and hearing that absurd business of the keys, would have told anybody a man had been in the shelter. When we got down to it, a child could have seen where the broken orchid had been cut off—and the trail of broken orchids leading away. When we got inside I saw at a glance that somebody had been in there."

He paused, to count another twenty, no doubt.

"And furthermore, my dear Mrs. Latham," he said, with a kind of iron self-control. *"Before* I came there, I knew a man had been hidden in the shelter, and I knew you were in absolutely no danger . . . and I knew who the man was."

19

I SUPPOSE I LOOKED AT HIM AS IF I REALLY were a complete fool.

He pulled a chair over and sat down in front of me.

"—And to think," he said, ruefully, "that I know you as well as I do and I still let you spoil a year's work for me . . ."

I was quite speechless.

"Some day, my dear, you'll give me credit—not much, just a little—for some rudimentary professional intelligence. You ought to have known I wouldn't conceivably have let you down like that unless I had a reason. I couldn't let those people know we knew Cather was there."

He drew another long breath, got up and paced around the little room.

"All I needed was for you to mind your sweet business and let mine alone. Listen, Mrs. Latham. I'd been working on this case for months. I knew who Roy Cather was—and a damned unprepossessing fellow."

That much, at least, I knew, very well.

"I knew he was trying to get—from Japan—to Honolulu. I knew somebody swam ashore Saturday night about nine-thirty from a Jap submarine. I knew Cather was a celebrated swimmer. The planes spotted a man, Sunday afternoon. I was in the one that did. When I saw it was a white man in a jungle suit making toward the Cathers' place, I knew it was Roy Cather. We did everything we could to help him get there—kept people out of his way and so on. He got there, to that jungle back of the Cathers' garden—Sunday evening."

I didn't even have to close my eyes to see that chalky-white and stubbly-dark face, so oddly frightening against the trees.

"We didn't pick him up, in spite of the fact that he'd killed a sentry on the beach. We wanted, of course, to see what he'd do. I'd been building this up, stone by stone, for months. We wanted to know who he was going to see and what he was trying to do. And now . . ." Colonel Primrose shrugged. ". . . he's dead."

I managed to speak, this time, and if I sounded meek it was the basest kind of deception. I was now getting madder still.

"Is that my fault too?" I asked.

"Yours and Mary Cather's. He thought he was safe till you locked him in the shelter. He'd made a deal with Alice Cather, I imagine. When he was cornered he had to act. The minute he acted, somebody else had to act too. He was killed. If you'd only let him alone——"

"You should have told me," I said.

"I couldn't tell you."

He sat down again.

"I'm in Army Intelligence. They make the rules. They don't go around taking half-witted civilians into their confidence. There's a war, Mrs. Latham. It's no game of cops and robbers."

"What was I supposed to do, then?" I demanded. "Wait around and get my throat cut? I may be half-witted, but I'm brighter than that."

He groaned.

"What possible interest were you to him, Mrs. Latham? There was no question of getting your throat cut."

"It didn't look that way to me with Roy Cather in my room with a knife in his hand," I said bitterly.

He was starting to get up and pace again, but he stopped.

"—What did you say?"

"Exactly what you heard. Maybe he was just going to sharpen a pencil, but that's not what it looked like to me, in the middle of the night. When I saw the Japanese houseman bringing him food on a silver tray maybe I should have got up and drawn him a bath. But I just have no way of knowing these things. He looked dangerous to me, and Mary and I had a naïve idea we were doing a patriotic duty. And anyway, how do *you* know all this? How do you know when he got there, and what he was doing?"

He was looking at me thoughtfully and with not quite so much distaste.

"That happens to be my business," he said quietly. "We have agents."

He hesitated. "I don't mind telling you we've had one on the Cather place a long time, knowing Roy Cather would try to get back. We were sure he was going to, after the broadcast from Tokyo."

I looked at him skeptically. If he had an agent on the place he was equipped with a magic hat that made him invisible to mortal eyes. Alice Cather, of course, had told Uncle Roy that I was it. I wondered suddenly if it could be Alice herself.

"Who is your agent?" I asked blandly.

"I can't tell you."

"What was the broadcast? Can you tell me that?"

He nodded. "It was to Alice Cather. She was in Washington then. It said, 'The Cardinal will call soon. Be at home.' It was picked up by monitors and amateurs all over the country. I saw her on Massachusetts Avenue and she pretended she hadn't heard it, but she was terrified. And that's when she decided to come home. No cardinal called on her in Washington."

I thought with some triumph that I might be half-witted but I was at least ahead of him on something.

"One did here," I said.

He looked at me as if he thought I'd lost my mind. "I beg your pardon?"

"I said, one did here. He meant a redbird."

"A redbird? Oh, you mean——"

"A cardinal, a bird with red feathers. That was his signal. I heard it when she did. She was scared out of her wits. That's how I got in it in the first place."

He sat there looking at me—narrowly, I believe it's called.

"I should have thought your agent would have told you," I added, not without malice. "And about Kumumato cutting the phones off, and about Roy Cather's daughter——"

He cut me off. "We know all about that. The phones from the house and the shelter have been under observation. He called the house, and he called his daughter. She went up and got a message he slipped under the door to her. We have the message. He ordered her to go to Mrs. Cather and have her unlock the door and let him out. And Corinne didn't do it. She went home and reported him to G2. At once, I may say. She turned him in before the man we sent to check on her got there."

"How patriotic," I said. "Or was it? Why did she?"

It just didn't make sense to me. I suppose I should have admired her loyalty, but somehow, what with her barging in on the Cathers and the story she'd told Swede, it sounded to me more like the fine old Order of the Double Cross.

"Does she know he's dead?" I added.

"Not to my knowledge," he said. "She probably thinks Army Intelligence has him. The reason she reported him is obvious. In the first place, get it out of your head that the Japanese and part Japanese in these Islands are on the side of Japan. Most of them are loyal citizens and have proved it. They know too much about Japan to want to be slave labor for their emperor. And Corinne . . . well, she would have been running an awful risk helping to hide him. I don't know how she feels about her father. I know how I feel about him. Anyway, she turned him in—in great haste."

"That's . . . funny," I said.

"I don't think so."

I let that pass. "And I suppose Kumumato's a fine, loyal, upstanding citizen too. I suppose he didn't know who he was taking food to, in the middle of the night. Or why he polished up the air-raid shelter. Or——"

"He knew who he was taking food to," Colonel Primrose said calmly. "He didn't polish up the shelter."

"Who did, then?"

"The fingerprints on the under side of the table and chairs are Mrs. Bronson's."

"Oh," I said. I sat there, trying to put two and two together. The only thing Colonel Primrose hadn't seemed to know about was Roy Cather in my room. And Alice Cather did know it . . . and it was the only thing Kumumato didn't know . . .

It dawned slowly on me who the invisible agent on the Cather place was.

Colonel Primrose smiled a little at the look on my face, and nodded.

"I expected you'd guess that sooner," he said blandly.

"Would you think we'd help Roy Cather get to a place where there was a Japanese we weren't absolutely sure of?"

I shook my head, trying to make more of the basic two plus two.

"Kumumato," he said, "has a law degree and he's a public accountant. He worked for a firm with offices in Tokyo and travelled back and forth a good deal. Roy Cather had become a Japanese subject, out of our jurisdiction—one of those people who thought the Japanese culture was superior. He had a Japanese wife under Japanese law. His function for the Japanese was to interpret this country to them. Kumumato kept in touch with him. He told Kumumato he'd be back when there was a war . . . and the Japs placed Kumumato with the Cathers again. In a sense, at any rate—they bombed him out on the 7th, incidentally killing his daughter, so he could move up there without attracting any particular attention."

"And Corinne?"

Colonel Primrose shrugged. "Roy Cather misunderstood her too. He thought both of them loved Japan, as he did, and hated America, as he did. I assure you, Mrs. Latham, she's been checked again and again."

I sat there a little disconcerted, all my spies evaporating like mist before my eyes.

"But," I said, "how do you account for her coming up to the Cathers, the way she's done?"

"—A purely personal matter between her and the

Cathers," he said quite suavely. "None of the Army's business. She'd have been up there long ago if she'd known she could. That was what her father told her last night. It was his threat against Alice Cather."

I remembered then Alice Cather saying, "And *she's* not coming here," when Mary and I were listening to them through the open door.

"—It's no concern of mine," Colonel Primrose said.

"Is murder any concern of yours?" I asked. I wouldn't, even at that point, have given three cents for Corinne Farrell's survival value if she stayed on up at the Cathers' house. I could feel it in the air, the way I'd felt it when she stood in the doorway asking her Aunt Alice where her bags should be put. And Colonel Primrose misunderstood me the way Uncle Roy, apparently, did the local Japanese.

"It is a concern of mine," he said gravely. "The murder of that kid on the beach, for instance, that Roy Cather can't be called on to answer for now. And his own murder, in a special sense. But it won't be hard to find out who did that. There weren't many people there. The three boys in the cottage, you, Corinne, Kumumato's family, Mrs. Bronson, Alice Cather, Harry, Mary. That's the lot."

"Harry didn't even know he was there," I said.

"He's out, then. It gets down to fewer still. You consider opportunity, and motive. The motive behind this is the only real interest it has."

He walked over to the window and stood looking

out for a moment. I could see the large figure of his guard, philosopher and friend outside, polishing the field tan car.

"It's all very discouraging," he said at last. "I got you over here because I thought you'd be around the Cathers and go the places they went, and get an outside view of what Kumumato reported inside. I guessed wrong all the way around. All I've got left is a simple case of murder. If you'd only minded your own affairs, my dear . . ."

He turned around. "Don't look so violent," he said. "I may have been a little unjust. But you're the most exasperating woman I've ever known. God knows why I'm in love with you. I don't. But that's what I asked you to come down here and have dinner with me to tell you . . . before we knew Cather was dead. I didn't realize until I saw you this morning how much I'd missed——"

A crashing noise came through the front door. I thought at first one of the giant carriers we could see over the roof top had emptied the bilge water. But I should have known it was just Sergeant Buck clearing his throat. I never thought I'd be glad to see his face again, but actually I was delighted. Colonel Primrose was not. He was the color of a molten brick, and for the first time in all the years I'd known them he turned on his sergeant violently.

"Will you get the hell out of here?" he said.

It was the uniform, surely. Sergeant Buck raised one large iron fist in a salute. "Yes, sir," he said rigidly.

Colonel Primrose turned back to me.

"I asked you down here because I want to ask you to marry me," he said.

Men are strange people. Of all the times he could have asked me to marry him when I would possibly have been delighted to say yes, he picked the one when I was still seething with indignation, with a full catalog of the wrongs I'd suffered at my tongue's tip —and having just been called a half-wit. All the other things he could say would just go in one ear and out the other. He'd called me a half-wit.

"No," I said. I said more, but No is all that mattered. It gave me enormous pleasure to say it, and it gave me more still, a couple of hours later, to decline to be driven back to the Cathers by Sergeant Buck, meek as he then was.

We were coming out of the officers' club. I had been fed and given orders to keep my mouth firmly shut about the fact that Roy Cather was dead or found or both.

"Buck will take you back. I've got work to do in Bethel Street," Colonel Primrose said.

But I'd spotted Tommy Dawson. He was over at the little grass shack where they dispense one bottle of luau juice a week to officers on the canteen list. He'd been to the post office too. He had a large batch of letters sticking out of his pocket.

Colonel Primrose saw him too. "What are you doing down here?" he asked.

Tommy paid for his bottle and came across to us.

"Collecting the mail and laying in a little rat poison, sir," he said cheerfully. "Coming up now, Grace?"

I nodded.

"Come on, then. You better come too, Colonel. We're going to have a murder up there tonight. Right down your alley. We're drawing straws. Only a sawbuck to enter."

Somehow, when it happened it didn't seem quite so funny. If indeed, I thought, Tommy meant it to be funny . . . if he wasn't in some curious kind of way telling Colonel Primrose he really ought to come.

"Well, she's got him, now," he said. "The big Swede." We were going up Nuuanu Avenue on the Pali road. "She spilled the dirt. Now that he knows Mary's all he ever cared about, he's got to pay up—just to make her keep her trap shut. It's a lousy deal."

He didn't say what dirt she'd spilled.

"Even if she shuts up till she gets the big Swede tied, sealed and delivered, I don't see anything to keep her shut up, do you?"

I shook my head.

"It'd sure be too bad if she accidentally slipped and fell over the Pali tonight, wouldn't it?" he said deliberately. "—It would be a damn shame, wouldn't it?"

But Corinne didn't slip and fall over the Pali. And there was no possible question of accident when they found her.

20

TOMMY DEPOSITED HIS BOTTLE OF LUAU juice, sardonically known in these parts as Black Death, in the cottage and came back to the car. The rain had stopped and the night was lovely, the sky above the black jagged rim of the mountains clear and luminous.

Down in the house Aunt Norah was sitting alone in the living room, her knitting idle in her lap, her head erect, back rigid, staring off into some very far distance. She began knitting instantly when she saw us.

"They're downstairs," she said curtly.

"Okay, Madame Defarge," Tommy said, after he'd closed the door, however, and we were going down to the game room.

Alice Cather and Harry weren't there, but the other four were, playing bridge. It was a curious sight, Mary's bright golden head, Corinne's sleek black one, Swede, large and blond and weatherbeaten, and Dave Boyer lean and taut—all of them silent at one of those friendly games where the players are determined to be polite or bust. Whatever the upheaval had been that had sent her flying back to the house, Corinne had recovered. She had a fixed, confident and a little insolent smile on her lips, and her small soft hands fluttered daintily with the cards.

Tommy leaned over the bannister and regarded them with an ironic grin. "Hi, friends.—Mail call. Catch it, David."

He tossed a whole batch of letters down to Dave.

"Just one for the Swede. It almost got on out forward. Came in a fat cat with a load of brass. It's from your old man."

He shied it over to Swede. It went wide and landed by the outside door. Swede went after it.

I've never seen a bridge game break up so willingly, at least on the part of three-fourths of the table. It looked as if they had been waiting in mutual agony for some excuse.

"Read your mail, children," Mary said. She gathered up the cards. "There's some Scotch, Tommy." She went over to the door to the service quarters. "Ice, please, Kumumato, and some ginger ale."

I wondered if now that his job was over he'd quietly pack and go back to his own business, leaving the Cathers, like everybody else in Honolulu, hunting frantically for a cook. I had the bizarre idea that maybe that was the way they'd get rid of Corinne. She'd no doubt take a dim view of helping with the housework, even in a house where her mother had learned the domestic ropes à l'Américaine.

Kumumato put the tray on the bamboo bar, his face as unrevealing as when he'd stood by and heard the

captain calling Corinne a slant-eyed Mata Hari. She'd
taken a deck and was dealing solitaire, apparently ob-
livious to the fact that she was about as popular as a
bunch of kahili flower, which is Hawaii's virulent ver-
sion of the Mainland's poison oak and used by apparently reputable florists in lavish bouquets for innocent
tourists.

Mary and Tommy were by the bar, Dave had
slumped down on the sofa, grinning over his mail.
Swede had opened his father's letter. A curious well
of silence seemed to envelop him, so tangible that Mary
and Tommy and I looked over at him all at the same
time. His face was very strange, as if it were frozen,
stunned into complete immobility by the news he was
reading. He finished the last page and just sat, staring
through it onto the floor. Then he got up, unaware
of any of us, and went out, walking slowly across the
garden.

"It's his aunt," Tommy said quietly. "The A. T. C.
pilot that brought it told me she had a stroke. She
always looked like an old sour puss to me, but she
thought the Swede was the white-haired angel child.
I guess he must have thought she was okay too. You
knew her, Grace."

I nodded. She was my next-door neighbor. I'd been
expecting her to have a stroke for years, every time
Sheila, my Irish setter, and her aged yapping Peke had
a boundary dispute at the tree in front of our houses.
I wouldn't have thought, however, that her emanation
could have stretched so far. The atmosphere was com-

pletely changed. It hung around us, heavy as sable
lead. Dave stopped reading and looked up. Swede had
gone out of the light from the door and was standing
at the top of the steps leading down to the pool, motionless, his hands in his pockets, his head bent forward.
Inside we sat silent for a moment, distressed for him.

"—Hey, Swede," Tommy called.

He moved like a man summoned from a long distance, shook himself, turned and came slowly along
the lighted rectangle. For a face that was hard-bitten
and stubborn and not made to show emotion, it was
extraordinary how much was there, etched deeply in
the rugged lines of his mouth and jaw. He came into
the room. It was Mary he was looking at. He stood
looking at her, not seeing any of the rest of us.

"Swede," Mary said. She started toward him, and
remembered. "What is it?"

He came over to her. He put his hand under her
chin, lifted her face up, and looked down into her
bewildered eyes.

"You didn't let me down, after all, did you, Mary?"
he said. It was hard to believe Swede's voice could be
so gentle and so tender. "I was a damned fool. I should
have known. Forgive me, will you, Mary?"

"I . . . don't know what you mean," she said.

He stood looking down at her for a moment.

"I'll read you this," he said then. "You can all listen.
It's from my old man."

He read the letter.

"Dear Son,—Joe's here in the office and is taking this out to you.

"Your aunt had a light stroke Thursday evening and sent for me. She couldn't talk clearly but I don't think there was much she could say.

"What was on her mind, thinking she was going to die, was three shoe boxes of letters in her secretary drawer. They were your letters to Mary Cather and hers to you. You had better trusted the post office. There was a note there your aunt must have written when her conscience began seriously troubling her. I won't send it on. It says that she worshipped you and couldn't see you ruin your life by a war-time marriage to a girl you scarcely knew and whose background nobody knew anything about. There's more but that's the gist of it. I might bring myself to feel sorry for her —her remorse is pathetic—except for the hash I understand you're making of your life at present. But after all this I wouldn't presume to try to advise you. I can also see what Mary must have felt, never hearing from you either. I tried to call her, but they've left Washington. There's nothing else to say. I can't even find it in my heart to say your aunt meant well—as I've often said in the past.

"The letters are here in my safe. Tell me what to do with them.

"Your aunt is better today. We're well. Your mother is writing. All our love.—Dad."

He read the letter through without a pause. Mary

stood unchanging as a statue of alabaster. Neither
Tommy nor Dave moved, nor did I. Corinne listened
a moment, and deliberately went on with her solitaire.
Swede folded the letter and put it in his pocket. He
and Mary looked at each other, silently. I think neither
of them could trust himself to speak, with words, if
indeed they had any need of words. The silence was
so long prolonged that Corinne put down her cards.
She pushed her chair back and got up, facing us all,
a startling gleam of triumph shining out of her dark
burning eyes.

"And what are you going to do about it?"

Swede looked at her steadily, his eyes hardening.
Mary looked at her too.

"It's . . . nice to know, Corinne," she said gently.
"It's nice to know there . . . there wasn't any malice
in it. She didn't mean to hurt us, ourselves."

The color rose sharply in Corinne's glowing peach-
bloom cheeks. Malice was all too plainly written in
every line of her body. The dark fire shot out of her
blazing brilliant eyes.

"—I tell you," she said. "I don't like you, sister.
I hate your straw-colored yellow hair, and your washed-
out blue eyes and——"

"Come, come, sister," Tommy said easily. "If you
don't mind your manners there's a little band of brothers
going to break your bloody neck——"

"Shut up, both of you," Swede said. He'd moved
into Dave's role, and Dave seemed to have retired. He

was sitting in his corner, looking with fixed eyes into the fireplace in front of him.

"You've said your say, Corinne," Swede said. "Be careful you don't say too much."

It was amazing to me that the girl could stand there, so sure of herself, so unaffected by the waves of something more inexorable than fury that spread out toward her. Hatred was not it either, or contempt. It was too involved and too . . . cold-blooded for any single word I know.

The telephone was ringing through the door in the servants' quarters. We heard it without paying attention till Kumumato came in.

"Excuse me, please. The phone is for you, Mrs. Farrell. This way, if you please."

But Corinne had turned on him, curiously enough. She broke into a rapid burst of words, highly voluble and excited. I saw Mary's eyes widen and her lips part. And Kumumato began to jabber too, as excitedly as Corinne. He broke off abruptly and said in English, "The telephone is waiting, Mrs. Farrell."

She slammed the door behind her.

"Well, what did they say?" Tommy asked. He calmly poured himself a large amount of Scotch. "Do you know, Mary?"

Mary didn't speak for a moment, and when she did it was a little unsteadily. "I . . . used to know a little Japanese. She . . . she was just telling him what she thinks of us. And he was telling her to be careful."

Tommy raised his glass.

"Here's to us just the same. It's a nice night out. Swede, why don't you and Mary take a walk. Dave and me and Grace will go and get stinko. Want to, Grace—do you good?"

I shook my head, a little reluctantly.

Swede and Mary looked at each other, and she shook her head, smiling. He took hold of her hand. "Come on, just for a minute. We've got to talk to each other. Please!"

They went out. Tommy put his head down on his folded arms on the bar for an instant. "Cripes," he said. He raised his head, drained his glass and put it down. "Come on, David," he said. "We've got a job to do."

I was alone there when Corinne came back. She'd been gone a long time, at least for an ordinary telephone conversation, it seemed to me. I also thought the peach-bloom looked a little faded. Her face was a compact tight little mask out of which her eyes shone, bright and sultry hot. She looked around the all but empty room.

"Where is Swede?"

"He and Mary have gone for a walk," I said.

She started toward the terrace, stopped abruptly and stood for a moment, and came back.

"They can't frighten me," she said. "I am not leaving here. I am staying. If my father is dead, they killed him."

I looked at her quickly. It was information newly come by, and I wondered where she'd got it. I'd been told not to say anything, and Kumumato would have been told the same.

"And it doesn't matter whether he is dead or not. They don't dare put me out. You'll see. I'll fix them. If I'd only known earlier what fun I could have had. And old Norah up there, trying to buy me off. Ha, ha."

"Look," I said. "Why don't you release Swede? You don't love him any more than he does you?"

She looked at me, smiling ever so faintly.

"Love him? No. I don't even like him. He feels sorry for me—I think so. Ha! He so sorry for poor little Corinne. He's a big fool."

"I think so too," a voice said.

Swede was standing there by the terrace opening. His face was white and lined with cold fury.

"You couldn't be more right," he said. "If you'll excuse me, Grace. I'm going up to see the Cathers."

The girl got up quickly, her face a pasty yellow.

"You be careful, Swede. You be careful what you say."

"If I were you I'd go to bed," Swede said quietly.

He went up the stairs. She stood for all the world like a sleek jungle cat momentarily at bay. Then she relaxed and shrugged.

"No," she said. "He wouldn't dare. They are fools. They would rather keep on telling lies to each other. I think so."

Kumumato came in from the service quarters. He went to the bar and began gathering up the glasses. Corinne spoke to him. She interrupted herself at once.

"Do you speak Japanese, Mrs. Latham?"

"No, I don't," I said.

She smiled at me and went on talking.

I said good night and started upstairs. Instead I went out onto the terrace. Mary was there, sitting on the top of the steps leading down to the terrace where the shelter was, looking vacantly off into the woods beyond the ravine. I sat down beside her.

"He's going to marry her," she said after a while. "I don't think he ought to—not for the reason he's doing it. He doesn't know I know it—but I do. That's what Corinne was telling Kumumato. He's an Intelligence agent. She told him she knew that, that was why she is safe up here. Then she told him what her father had told her. That's when he interrupted her. It's funny, isn't it?"

"Not very," I said.

"It is, in a way—Swede marrying her because he loves me. Oh, I hate her. I never thought I'd hate her, or anybody. But I could kill her. What right has she to ruin everybody's life this way?"

"You'd better come along and go to bed, angel," I said. "Tomorrow everything'll look different."

Any other time—and it was on the tip of my tongue right then—I'd have said, "We'll get hold of Colonel Primrose." But he'd already washed his hands of these affairs. "—Purely personal . . . none of the Army's business." I wondered suddenly. Swede's commanding officer could stop his marriage to Corinne. He couldn't, however, I thought immediately, stop Corinne.

Above us on the lanai I was dimly aware of quiet unhurried voices talking in the dark. I looked up. Outlined in the soft glow of light from inside the house was Swede's large bulky figure, bulkier because Alice Cather was on one side of him and Harry on the other. Norah Bronson was there by her brother, and the four of them were talking earnestly. Their voices stopped. Corinne was coming out of the game room, a single white-clad figure on the bare green stage made by the rectangle of light from the open wall of the room behind her.

She stood perfectly still a moment. Whether she was aware of the audience she had in the dark periphery I have no idea. She stood motionless for a long time, and then raised both arms, stretching them up to that inverted bowl we call the sky. Then she laughed, a liquid silver peal of laughter, long and lingering, and eerie beyond words. It stopped as abruptly as it had begun. She let her arms drop to her sides and turned. She did a slow melting hula movement, raising her butterfly hands again, moving her hips gracefully, back into the game room . . . leaving her stage still lighted, but as silent, and as silent all around it, as if the lights had been switched off, leaving it in total blackness. And no audience was ever as silent as the one she'd left just then.

I went to bed. Mary went out on the lanai and sat

down in the bamboo chaise longue. I picked up a book,
but I'd never felt less like reading and I put it down.
I switched off the light and left her sitting there in
the dark. When I went to sleep she was still there.
She wasn't, however, when I woke up, and her bed
next to mine was still smooth and unrumpled.

I didn't know at first what had waked me, but I
was as clearly and completely awake as if I'd not been
asleep at all. I looked at the clock. It was nearly half-
past two. The hurried tick-tick-tick racing the seconds
along was perfectly audible in the dense blanket of
silence lying heavily all around it. I listened intently.
Other sounds seeped up—the muted drip-drip of the
shower head behind the closed door of the bathroom,
the far-off sound of the water tumbling along the bottom of the ravine, the wind softly stirring somewhere
in the trees . . . and my own heart, beating with a
suddenly vague but paradoxically acute anxiety.

I put the covers back and got up. I remember wondering, absurdly, who it was who said "I should of
stood in bed," and whether they weren't the famous last
words of somebody. Though they hardly applied, because in nothing flat all hell broke loose in the house
there in the hills.

21

WHEN I SAY ALL HELL BROKE LOOSE I MEAN
some one started to scream, and kept on. It was a
woman, and it was more of a shriek than a scream.
It echoed, high-pitched and terrible, through the walls,
hitting the side of the mountain and bounding back
again, lingering on even after it was cut abruptly off
at the source, reverberating through the new and sudden silence. They must have heard that scream at
Kaneohe Bay and as far up as Kuhuku, or perhaps in
Molokai and Maui. It was unbearably blood-curdling
and terrifying—and that it was Corinne was as clear
in my mind as daylight. And suddenly everybody was
running. I was running and there were running feet
all over the place.

I still didn't know what had waked me. It wasn't
the scream, because I'd been out of bed then for
minutes . . . it seemed, and it must have been at least
one. But it didn't seem to matter much, and I ran along
the shadowy lanai, turned the corner and came to a
stop that nearly threw me off balance. Some one was
there near me, in the living room. I couldn't tell
whether coming out or going in, because whoever it

was was standing there, motionless. Then a white blur materialized.

"Alice!" I gasped. "What is it?"

She moved back without answering, almost stealthily, as if trying to get away without speaking.

"*Alice!*"

"Sssh!" she said. "I . . . I don't know. It must be down there. Go on and see. I'll come in just a minute."

She disappeared into the living room. I still didn't know whether she'd come that way or the other . . . from where Corinne had screamed and where it was quiet, dreadfully quiet, now.

I went on, around the corner of the living room. The service door was open and a path of light shining out of it cut sharply across the lanai. Huddled in the stairway, clutching in abject terror at each other, were the two little Japanese maids and their grandmother, Kumumato's wife. I hurried on toward the next path of softer, dimmer light that came out from Mary's room. Then I slowed down and stopped, and caught hold of the redwood rail.

The voice I heard, low and insistent, was Harry Cather's.

"—Be quiet, Norah. For God's sake be quiet."

I stood there, getting my breath, listening.

"Call the police, Kumumato. Don't touch anything. Just call the police . . . and do it, don't stand there like a damned idiot."

I knew then that it wasn't Corinne who had screamed.

It was Norah Bronson. And I knew what it was that had waked me. It wasn't intuition that told me that. It was the smell of cordite. It was coming in faint but unmistakable swirls out of the room, dissolving in the cool mountain air. It was a shot that had waked me. The scream came after.

"Be quiet, Norah," Harry Cather said again.

I moved closer where I could see inside but not be seen myself unless they looked, and they would hardly bother to look just then. I saw the bed first. Just for an instant, before I looked away, I saw the bed, and I saw Corinne. I saw the monstrous stain where her throat had been. It was moving, alive and liquid and horrible. Her face above it was strangely gray, and above that the shiny black rim of her hair was grotesquely smooth and undisturbed. I looked away quickly, but I could still see it, and the others there, with a dreadful reality: Norah Bronson, Harry Cather, and Kumumato.

Harry Cather, his face white, his great brown eyes all that was alive in it, was gripping his sister's arm, trying to make her stop shaking and stop the strange noises in her throat. Kumumato was all shrunk together, as if the terror of it was too much. He had a blue kimono pulled around his shoulders above his pajama trousers, and as he went unsteadily to the door he looked almost as if he were crying, his head bent and shaking.

"—Use the study phone, keep the rest of them out

of here," Harry Cather said. When Kumumato had left he turned quickly to his sister. He seemed thinner and straighter than ever, his eyes brilliant and burning.

"Give it to me, Norah!" he said. "For God's sake, what were you thinking of?"

Her hand, concealed in the folds of her print dress, moved out. It held an automatic revolver, small, ugly, glittering, blue-black. His hand closed on it quickly.

"I only came to frighten her—that's all, Harry! I only came to frighten her. I was going to——"

He cut her off sharply. "Hand me the quilt. Now get out of here. Go in the living room. Pull yourself together. Get a drink. And quit shaking . . ."

He turned to the door. Alice Cather was there, in a yellow satin negligee, her hair rumpled, all her makeup washed off. She was obviously just out of bed.

"Get out of here, Alice," Harry said roughly. He barred her way so she could not see that bed, even with the silk quilt covering the silent figure on it. "Take Norah to the living room, and be quiet, both of you. I'll be there in a minute.—The police are coming."

He pushed Norah out and closed the door on the two of them. Then he stood there perfectly still for a moment, looking over at the bed and the figure on it under the quilt. His eyes moved quickly around the room, and he turned and went out.

I stood there too sick to move, my knees like heavy

water. The room in front of me, now that Harry Cather
had gone too, was terribly silent, and terribly empty.
On the floor between the bed and the threshold of
the lanai, Corinne's big red handbag was lying, part
open, its contents spilling out of it. A small gold compact, open, and the pink feather puff, stained brown
with face powder, had fallen out onto the mat. A newspaper lay on the floor, open as if she'd been reading
it and had thrown it aside. There was a large blotch
of blood on it. Her suitcase against the wall by the
bathroom door was pulled crazily half off the luggage
rack . . . as if, I thought, Norah Bronson had been
rummaging through it before the girl woke up.—But
chiefly there was that monstrous red stain, creeping up,
with dreadful accusing fingers, through the silk cover
they'd put over her . . . as though to say, *You can't
hide me—not with all the pink silk in the world you
can't hide me. I'm murder . . . murder most foul.*
It was dyeing the glossy sheen a sickening reddish-
brown.

There was a whisper behind me on the terrace. I
started violently and turned. It was Mary. Her face
was a white blur in the shadow. Beyond her light was
coming through the door where the two maids and
Kumumato's wife had huddled. They were gone now.
There was light in the living room, streaming in pale
segments where the walls were open onto the lanai.
I looked at Mary. It was all very strange. My mind

was like a crazy album of pictures that I was seeing all at the same time. Corinne . . . Harry's hand taking the gun from Norah. The bag, the paper with blood on it on the floor. And Mary. There was something very wrong about Mary. It came slowly into my mind that there was, but not what it was, until, down in the rectangle of light from the living room, I saw Alice Cather come out unsteadily and move over to the rail.

I looked at Mary again. She was dressed for bed too. She had on pajamas and a white bath-towel robe that came to her knees, tied around the waist with a green cord. Her hair was touselled as if she'd been in bed. But she hadn't. I could still see the unrumpled sheets and the chair with the robe and pajamas neatly folded over it.

"Is it true . . . what Kumumato said? She's dead?"

I nodded. Suddenly there was a sound of racing motors, cars coming. The yellow sweep of headlights slanted over the trees in the gully where the orchids were.

"Come, Grace," she whispered. "Come quickly—it's the police."

It was a new picture on top of the others, not blotting them out, leaving them clear as before through the startling clarity of this one superimposed. The living room flooded with light, the police—civilian police, brown-skinned, handsome, their uniforms sharply differentiating them from the lighter khaki of the men there from the Army's Criminal Intelligence. They were in the room, suddenly taking charge, stationed at the doors, herding us together, all of us, while around we could hear the tread of rapid feet, sharp commands given. We were all here. Harry Cather, lean and very tall in his pongee dressing gown. Norah Bronson rigidly erect in her chair and very pale, still in one of her old nondescript print dresses. Alice Cather sitting over on the lime-green and chartreuse yellow couch where the captain had sat the Sunday evening I arrived . . . ages and ages ago, it seemed. Her face and her hands in her lap were the color of the couch, only grayer-green. Her head was bent forward, her eyes closed. Kumumato had changed from the blue kimono and put on his white house jacket, starched and perfect above his pajamas. He stood by the door, his face pale, the beads of sweat standing out on his forehead.

The front door opened and Tommy and Dave came in. Tommy's red head was as wet as if they'd pulled him out of the shower, and his shirt was wet. So was Dave's. Behind them was Swede, his stubborn rugged jaw pale and set. He looked quickly over at Mary. She took a step toward him.

"Stay where you are, please."

The police officer turned to the boys. "Over here, gentlemen."

Another car had driven up. And for a moment my heart stopped its hammer-hammer and was still. Colonel Primrose came in, Sergeant Buck the traditional two paces behind him. They were both moving more rapidly than was traditional.

"Nothing has been touched, sir," somebody said.

Colonel Primrose's sparkling black eyes moved swiftly around the room without a gleam of recognition of any person he knew.

"This way, sir," one of the officers said.

Harry Cather moved. "I can tell you, Colonel Primrose——"

"Thank you," Colonel Primrose said quietly. "Mr. Kumumato will come with me."

I heard the swift catch in Mary's breath as she sat by me on the sofa. Alice Cather raised her head sharply, Harry Cather's lips tightened to a thin straight line. Only Aunt Norah seemed not to hear. She sat rigid and erect as before, her eyes fixed on the wall ahead of her. It took an effort for me to remember that it was she who'd screamed and that it was her hand shaking as if with palsy as she'd given the gun to her brother. And Tommy and Dave looked at Kumumato, their jaws sagging a little before they glanced at each other and then did an elaborate ritual of getting out cigarettes, as if what the hell, it didn't make any difference to them who the Colonel had help him. And the silent trio by the service door, the two little maids and Mrs. Kumumato, huddled together, their eyes big with fear.

I don't know how long it was we sat there. It seemed years to me as I listened, straining my ears to make out some intelligible syllable from the shadowy voices coming along the lanai. I could see them, in my mind, opening the door, stopping an instant, going to the bed. Was one of the men in uniform a surgeon? I didn't know, he could easily be. I could see them taking off the pink silk quilt . . . that would be the moment the voices stopped and there was complete silence for an instant. I kept on trying to follow them in my mind. Colonel Primrose picking up the red bag and the gold compact with the pink feather puff lying beside it, Sergeant Buck picking up the newspaper with the stain of blood . . . all of them sniffing the air, recognizing the smell of cordite . . .

I went through all of it, sitting there, but much too fast, because I'd followed them every step over the room and was through long before they were, in physical fact. Then I sat there, waiting . . . not daring quite to look at Aunt Norah, wondering what sentences she was framing to bring out later when they began to question her, what was going on in her mind.

Suddenly down the passage there was a small commotion, a quick raising of voices that still weren't clear enough to understand, a more hurried moving of feet. It was not very long after that that Colonel Primrose came back. Kumumato was behind him, and Buck behind him. They were all three tight-lipped, their eyes hard and intent. They brought a chill in with them . . . the kind that creeps into the human heart and numbs and paralyzes.

"Who fired this gun?" Colonel Primrose asked.

His voice was not loud, but it sounded like the report of a gun itself. He stood in the center of the room where we could see him, all of us, his hand out, the blue-black automatic lying in his opened palm.

22

"WHICH ONE OF YOU FIRED THIS?" HE RE-
peated deliberately.

I looked at the floor intently, terrified for fear I'd
unconsciously look across the room at the rigid old
woman in the print dress by the fireplace. Everything
that moved me seemed to be physically pulling at my
eyes to turn them that way.

"I believe none of us is bound to say anything that
would be self-incriminating, Colonel Primrose," Harry
Cather said. He turned, looking at him calmly. "—If
any one of us did fire it."

Colonel Primrose looked at the watch on his wrist.

"I'm merely trying to save time, Mr. Cather," he
said evenly. "The picture here is very clear indeed.
I'd like to save you all as much heartbreak as is possible, under the circumstances. Mr. Kumumato has been
in the house for some time. He is an Intelligence agent.
I already know everything that has been going on up
here. I've known it for several days. This is the second
murder that has taken place——"

Harry Cather was staring at him as if he had lost his mind. Alice started to get up, abruptly, and stopped, still staring at him, her lips gray. And I realized that the people who were not staring were the important ones—the ones who knew. Mary wasn't, nor Aunt Norah . . . Kumumato, Swede, Tommy, Dave, or myself. The three boys knew, then. I looked from one of them to the other, remembered quickly that I must not look at anybody there, and looked down at the floor. It was too easy to give away people, with Colonel Primrose watching all of us, his eyes moving everywhere in the room at once.

"I think no one need pretend surprise," he said, I thought a little dryly. "Roy Cather was murdered here night before last. His daughter has been murdered here tonight."

The room was so silent that a centipede crawling across the lau-hala matting would have sounded like a company of marching men.

"Roy Cather was murdered, and his body thrown into the ravine," he went on quietly. "Mr. Kumumato informed me at seven-forty-five that evening that Roy Cather had been locked in the air-raid shelter by Miss Cather. Mrs. Latham helped. Dawson here and Boyer acted as a guard of honor—unsuspecting, I imagine—in case there was trouble. Mr. Kumumato was directed to unlock the shelter and give Roy Cather as much reassurance as possible, and help him to escape . . . for reasons we need not go into here. He reported that he could not unlock the shelter. In the meantime, Mrs. Cather——"

He turned to Alice, sitting motionless and white.

"In the meantime, you, Mrs. Cather, telephoned Mrs. Bronson."

He turned to Aunt Norah then.

"You telephoned to Mrs. Bronson, at her hotel, asked her if she had her key to the shelter, and asked her to bring it up at once. Which you did, Mrs. Bronson."

Aunt Norah made no sign that she was aware he was talking either to or about her.

"You not only brought your key up here," Colonel Primrose continued evenly. "You went to the shelter *alone*, Mrs. Bronson, and unlocked it. Mrs. Cather did not go with you. Why, Mrs. Bronson?"

Aunt Norah looked up at him then, very steadily.

"I have no idea what you're talking about, Colonel Primrose." She said it without batting a single eyelash. "Roy Cather is in Tokyo, to the best of my meager knowledge. I have never pretended to keep track of him or his doings."

Colonel Primrose put his hand in his blouse pocket and took out an envelope. He opened it deliberately. He took out a small jagged piece of purple and white printed silk, and laid it calmly on the table beside him, under the bright yellow light from the Chinese lamp. Mrs. Bronson's eyes were fixed on it. She said nothing, and Colonel Primrose made no comment. He went on equably.

"We have checked a telephone call made from the air-raid shelter to you in Maui, on Sunday night at ten-eighteen o'clock, Mrs. Bronson. Roy Cather called you then. He told you he was here, that he was coming to stay with you shortly, that you were to have a place ready for him."

"Nonsense," Norah Bronson said.

"And yesterday morning, early, you sent your purple and white print dress to the cleaner. It's in our possession at present. It has dried blood on it, Mrs. Bronson, that you attempted to wash out but missed in several places."

He looked down for an instant at the tiny piece of silk on the table.

"And this piece of that dress caught on the money belt that Roy Cather wore under his shirt. We found it there when we found his body. It was caught there when you dragged his body to the side of the ravine and pushed it over, Mrs. Bronson."

Aunt Norah looked at him. for a long instant. Her face darkened.

"Roy Cather was a traitor and a spy," she said harshly. "He deserved a worse death than he got."

Her eyes met Colonel Primrose's steadily, and there was no tremor in her voice.

"I have no sympathy with this coddling of prisoners and spies and traitors. I have long since forgotten that Roy Cather's parents and mine were the same."

Her voice rose.

"Even if I were to be hanged, Colonel Primrose, I'd have done the same thing. But I don't think any jury in the Islands will do anything but say 'Well done.' I don't expect them to hang me."

Colonel Primrose looked at her curiously. "Then may I ask why you went to all the trouble of cleaning up the air-raid shelter?"

"I like things neat. And I cleaned up after Roy Cather the way you'd clean up after a polecat in the cellar."

She looked him squarely in the face. "If you're trying to get me rattled, Colonel Primrose, you may as well stop. I'm an old woman and I'm a tough one."

Colonel Primrose smiled a. little.

"—Which brings up another point, Mrs. Bronson," he said very suavely. "Why did you scream, just now, when you—or some one—shot Corinne Farrell? Kumumato heard some one scream. He came running up from downstairs. He found you there, still screaming violently. Is that correct?"

"It's quite correct.—Lieutenant Ellicott, my knitting, please, there by your chair. Don't be frightened, Colonel, there's nothing dangerous in it."

I heard, still trying not to look at her, the click-click of the needles.

"As for Corinne Farrell," Norah Bronson said a little more quietly, "I do not think they will hang me for shooting her, either."

Colonel Primrose looked at her intently, giving the

impression as he does of also looking intently at every
one else in the room at the same time.

"I'm inclined to agree with you about that, Mrs.
Bronson," he said politely. His black eyes did move
then from face to face around the room, and back to
Aunt Norah. "And for at least one very good reason.
There are several reasons, no doubt. The first and most
important is that Corinne Farrell was not shot. She was
stabbed to death . . . stabbed to death with a knife."

That sank in as a rocket would sink in a plummet
dive down into the silent depths of the ocean. The
silence received it, and closed over it.

Colonel Primrose turned to the two officers standing at the top of the steps to the entrance hall.

"You'll find a knife here, somewhere," he said.
"You'll probably find it wrapped in pages 3–4 of this
evening's paper. There won't have been time enough
to get it far away. Begin at this end of the house and
find it."

He called them back when they had taken a step
or two.

"There are some shoes around here with face powder
on them. Have a look for them, and also for any
tracks."

It was all I could do to keep from raising my foot
to look at the bottom of my slipper, and I suppose
that was true of everybody in the room. But it wasn't
a sign of guilt, I told myself quickly, for I wasn't
guilty.

Colonel Primrose turned back to us.

"Where were you, Mr. Cather?"

"I was in my room in bed, asleep," Harry said. "I heard my sister scream, and ran in to see what was the matter."

"You heard nothing before your sister screamed?"

"I was asleep," Harry repeated. His face was very pale, but that, I thought, like the impulse to look for face powder on our shoes, was natural enough.

Colonel Primrose turned to the three boys sitting together against the wall.

"When you said there was going to be murder up here tonight, Dawson, this is what you had in mind?"

"No, sir," Tommy said. "Not exactly." He spoke without hesitation and very seriously. "I just figured you couldn't go on indefinitely asking for it without getting it. That's all."

"And where have you two been?" Colonel Primrose looked at their soaked shirts.

"Down in the gully looking at the orchids, sir," Tommy said. "—Wet, down there."

"What were you doing besides looking at the orchids, Lieutenant?"

"Preliminary reconnaissance, sir. Getting the lay of the land for future operations."

Dave Boyer moved impatiently. "Shut up, you fool," he said. "—We were figuring on putting the fear of the Lord in Corinne Farrell, sir. We were going to frighten her so she'd watch her step. That's all, sir.

That's as far as we got. We didn't get to her room.
We heard a shot, and somebody screamed. By the time
we got out of the gully back up on the road the cops
got us."

I remembered something suddenly. It might not
be one of the people here. It might have been some one
from the outside. I remembered the telephone call
she'd got, from some one she'd said was trying to
frighten her.

"And you, Ellicott?"

Mary Cather leaned forward quickly.

"He was with me, Colonel Primrose," she said.
"We were out by the pool, sitting there talking. It
seemed . . . it seemed like the last chance we'd have,
and we . . . we wanted to use it. We were there all
the time."

Colonel Primrose had not looked at her. His eyes
were still resting on Swede.

"Most of the time, sir," Swede said. He looked
across the room at Mary smiling at him. "Not all of
it. I came in to get a coat for Mary, out of the closet
in the game room. I went in the kitchen and got some
chicken out of the ice box for us. I was there when
Mrs. Bronson yelled."

I should have thought that massive as Sergeant Buck
is and conscious of his presence as I always am, I should
have noticed that he'd left. But I didn't, not till he
came back at that moment.

"Sir," he said stiffly. That was when I saw him
standing at the top of the two steps to the entrance

hall, bleak and stony-faced. He jerked his head and thumb simultaneously toward the passage behind him, that led toward my room and Alice Cather's.

Colonel Primrose hesitated an instant.

"Excuse me," he said. He followed Buck out. We sat there in silence till he returned.

"Mrs. Cather," he said, "—what were you doing this evening?"

Alice drew herself together. It was an effort, a really great one. It took several seconds before she seemed able to trust herself to speak.

"You don't have to answer," Harry Cather said. He went over and sat down beside her. "This is not a court of law."

Colonel Primrose nodded, his eyes not moving from Alice Cather's white face. "Right, Mr. Cather. It is not a court of law."

"It's all right, Harry." She put her hand out and took his. "I was writing letters. It . . . took a long time."

"When did you burn them, Mrs. Cather? And why?"

"You don't have to answer, Alice."

"I . . . don't have to answer, Colonel Primrose," she repeated.

"The ashes are still warm," Colonel Primrose said quietly. "I suggest you burned them when you knew Corinne Farrell was dead. Is that correct?"

She closed her eyes.

"You decided it was her life or yours, didn't you, Mrs. Cather?" he asked, almost gently.

She shook her head, and tried desperately to control her voice.

"—I didn't kill her."

"You were going to, weren't you?"

"I . . . perhaps," Alice said. Her voice was hardly audible. "I . . . I thought about it. I . . . there's no reason why I shouldn't be as frank as Norah. But I wouldn't have had the courage to . . . face a jury. I was going to finish it all the way around. Myself as well as her."

Harry Cather had put his arm around her and was holding her to his side.

"She doesn't know what she's saying, Colonel Primrose," he said patiently.

Colonel Primrose looked at them in silence for an instant, and turned back to the rest of us.

"I didn't expect any one of you to admit openly at this time that he killed Corinne Farrell," he said slowly. "One of you did. I tell you quite frankly, I know who it was. And I will tell you what happened. Mrs. Bronson has taken the blame for killing Roy Cather. I suppose she would be glad to take the blame for killing Corinne Farrell too. It happens that she did not kill either of them. She did throw Roy Cather's body over the ravine. And she did something else."

He turned to her.

"You didn't shoot Corinne, Mrs. Bronson. She wasn't shot.—Who did you shoot?"

23

AUNT NORAH DID NOT LOOK UP, BUT I
thought the clicking needles sounded less like knives
being sharpened than before.

"I couldn't say, Colonel. A shadow, possibly. I'm
a nervous woman. I didn't hit whatever it was. I'm a
bad shot."

It was not exactly a gasp that went up from the
three Cathers, but they weren't entirely able, I thought,
to conceal the fact that that last statement was not
true.

"You shot at something then. Before you turned
on the light?"

She nodded.

"You'd come there—like others, we're told—to
frighten the girl?"

Norah Bronson hesitated, and nodded. "Yes. I had."

"When you fired, in the dark—did you think it was
Corinne?"

There was only the slightest hesitation.

"I may have. I don't remember. I know I was very
much alarmed when I turned on the light and saw her
there."

"Let's go back a little, Mrs. Bronson. Roy Cather was dead, when you unlocked the shelter and found him there. That is true, isn't it?"

"He gave every indication of it," Mrs. Bronson said grimly. The needles stopped. Her eyes rested steadily on him, grave and suspicious.

"Between the time Mr. Kumumato informed me the shelter was locked and the keys gone from their usual place, and the time you unlocked the shelter and found him dead, some one had gone in and killed him. Some one he trusted——"

"Not necessarily, Colonel Primrose."

She interrupted him sharply.

"—You forget I had to clean the place up. There were signs of considerable struggle."

I thought Colonel Primrose looked at her with some surprise. And I couldn't keep from telling him what I'd thought of any longer.

"Have you thought that it might have been some one outside the house?" I asked. "Corinne got a telephone call this evening. It couldn't have been from any one inside . . ."

Colonel Primrose smiled at me, with patient courtesy.

"It was from me," he said urbanely. "I told her her father was dead and her legal status—if any—was . . . changed. I advised her to leave at once. She said she would. I take it something changed her mind."

It might have been the fact of knowing that Swede and Mary were out there in the garden together, I thought. And of course she probably had no real in-

tention of going . . . knowing then that Kumumato
had a semi-official status and depending on it to protect
her. I didn't say that, however, not wanting to call any
more attention to Swede and Mary than there already
was. I said, "Oh, I'm sorry."

The officers Colonel Primrose had sent out to find
the knife Corinne had been killed with appeared in the
doorway.

"—The knife is not in the house, sir," one of them
said. "—Unless it is in this room."

I can't describe the silence then. It was intensely
alive . . . electric and vibrant, and as unlike the silence
that descended in Corinne's room after Harry Cather
had closed the door behind him as midnight is unlike
high noon. And for all of my life I could not help
looking at Aunt Norah's knitting bag. And I simply
tore my eyes away, and looked steadily at Colonel
Primrose. That, at least, I knew was safe.

Colonel Primrose nodded very calmly.

"You see, Mrs. Bronson," he said, "while you are
not the murderer yourself, you do happen to be the
key to this whole affair. From the beginning you have
been protecting some one. I don't know whether you
have thought you were protecting one person, or two
persons . . . but you have been trying, desperately,
to shield the person or persons who killed Roy Cather
and his daughter. And I should have thought there
was only one person in this room that you'd go as far
as you have gone to protect.

"The person we're talking about is the one who got

the shelter keys away from Mrs. Latham, unlocked the shelter, killed Roy Cather, returned the keys to their proper places where Mr. Kumumato found them . . . after you, Mrs. Bronson, had thrown his body into the ravine and cleaned the place up.—I assume, by the way, that Mrs. Cather helped you clean it up?"

Aunt Norah nodded, grim-faced and silent.

"And so," Colonel Primrose went on, "the keys were returned, Mr. Kumumato found the shelter empty and in order, and so notified me."

I stared at him, trying not to think at all. It couldn't have been Alice herself . . . it couldn't have been.

"And it was this same person who drove the knife into Corinne Farrell's throat, Mrs. Bronson—who was in her room, just leaving it, when you opened the door . . . and at whom you shot, not knowing who it was. And then you tried to save that person, when you found out what had happened . . . by attracting attention, deliberately, for as long a time as you could, to give the murderer of Corinne Farrell time for concealment. For you are not a screaming woman, Mrs. Bronson.—And I should have thought the only person in the world you'd lift a finger to save is . . . Mary Cather."

His eyes rested steadily on her for an instant before he added, "But of course it was not Miss Cather you shot."

I can't describe what new quality the silence in the room had then, as I became gradually aware—and I suppose all of us did except one person—of something that was happening there, right under our very eyes, as we held our breath. No one spoke or moved. I don't know when it had begun. It was advanced and all too horribly clear when I first became aware of it, and it was as audible as if it were loud, or shrieking. Yet it was silent, as silent as the liquid blood flowing noiselessly, noiselessly, from the severed carotid in Corinne Farrell's throat. It was there in the room with us. It was creeping along the web and the woof of the material covering it, creeping silently out . . . and shouting . . . shouting murder.

"For you didn't shoot at a shadow, Mrs. Bronson," Colonel Primrose said. There was no change in his voice at all. "And you are not a bad shot. You are well known to be a good one. You fired a single shot, and it went home."

It was still creeping, spreading, dark against shining white.

"You each had a motive, of a sort, for murder," Colonel Primrose said. "The motive that some of you had was urgent and driving. But . . . there are different motives. There are three motives, great and constantly compelling: gain . . . fear . . . revenge.

"And it was revenge that struck this blow," he said quietly. "I must ask you to take off your coat, Mr. Kumumato."

The blood was spreading slowly through the starched white fabric of the glistening mess jacket. Kumumato's

face was pale yellow. The sweat stood on it. He made
one futile gesture. Sergeant Buck stood there by his
side, a human Pali, rising sheer and rocky above him.

"Take off your coat, Mr. Kumumato," Colonel
Primrose said evenly. "And give me Roy Cather's
knife."

Kumumato's right hand moved slowly, unbuttoning
his coat. His left hand hung at his side. Sergeant Buck
reached down. His right hand grasped Kumumato's,
his left ripped the jacket open. He drew out something
wrapped in a sheet of newspaper, held in the cord
around Kumumato's waist.

"Roy Cather stole your wife, Mr. Kumumato,"
Colonel Primrose said. "All these years you've followed him for us, you've followed not for us but for
the time when you could do what you did the other
night. It was you who took the keys from Mrs. Latham's
bag. You locked the shelter again, after you had killed
Cather. You planned to take his body away, to some
cave in the hills, perhaps. Mrs. Bronson was first. She
interrupted you tonight. She knew she had hit you.
She tried to give you time to bind up your arm."

The blue kimono, I thought . . . and he was
shrunken, going to the door, not from horror but from
pain.

"So she screamed, and everybody was concerned with
her and with Corinne while you could get out and
bandage your wound without anybody seeing you—because there was no way to silence the alarm the shot

at you had raised.—If you will raise your foot, Mr. Kumumato, you will find face powder on it. You were going through Corinne Farrell's bag when Mrs. Bronson disturbed you. You took half a dozen steps, leaving a trail of powder, on the lanai before she called you back. There will be blood on the floor that we can't see now. There's a spot in your bathroom where you reached across the tub to get a towel off the rack. You'd better go now, Mr. Kumumato, and let them dress your arm."

The rest of us sat or stood as we were.

"But why did he kill Corinne?"

I wasn't conscious that I was saying it aloud, and maybe I didn't. It may have been the concentrated power of a common thought in everybody's mind that made Colonel Primrose answer the question, spoken or unspoken. And he hesitated, for quite a while, before he went on, as if not quite sure of what he should say.

"Corinne Farrell had a piece of paper, twenty years or so old, that her father gave her. It was to be brought to Mrs. Cather, to make her let him out of the shelter. But Roy Cather didn't know his daughter. When she saw what he had given her she had no intention of releasing him. The paper could be used for her own devices. And Kumumato was trying to find it. He killed Roy Cather because he hated him. He killed his daughter partly because she was his daughter—and the daughter of the woman who left him—but mostly out of sheer friendship and loyalty to you, Mrs.

Cather. Because you've suffered in all this too . . ."

Colonel Primrose stopped and looked around at us all. Then his eyes rested on Norah Bronson, and he smiled a little.

"Well, what you said about a jury not hanging you, Mrs. Bronson, may apply to him even better. He's done an honorable job for us. It's a pity he couldn't have let the law do the rest of it."

When he'd gone Aunt Norah folded up her knitting.

"I am going to bed," she said, very calmly. "I advise the rest of you to do the same."

Alice Cather rose unsteadily. She crossed the room and put her arms around Norah Bronson's gaunt figure.

"Don't thank me," Aunt Norah said. "And he's wrong about one thing. I did *not* scream on account of Kumumato—I wouldn't trust one of them as far as I could see him in the dark. But I've never been able to bear the sight of blood. Good night. I'm leaving in the morning, and I still think you pay too much for the repairs you make around here, Harry."

Harry Cather came over to his wife and took her hand. "Why didn't you tell me he was here?" he asked quietly.

Alice shook her head. "I was afraid. Afraid you might kill him. I didn't want blood on . . . on your hands. Good night."

Swede Ellicott was by Mary's side. He put his arms around her and held her tightly for a moment. Then he bent down and kissed her on the forehead. "Tomorrow, Mary," he said. He turned and started out. "Come on, you goons," he said.

Mary stood there for a moment when we were alone, pale but with a radiant light shining in her eyes.

"He says it doesn't matter," she said. "He says it doesn't make any difference to us at all."

24

I DIDN'T KNOW WHAT SHE MEANT THEN. I
didn't know until morning, when I was in Alice Cather's sitting room. Harry Cather was there and Colonel
Primrose had come out.

In his hand Colonel Primrose held a small yellowed
piece of paper that he'd taken carefully from his bill-
fold. It was black and worn through along the edges
where it had been folded a long time.

"This is what Kumumato was looking for and didn't
find," he said. "She did have it with her. It was hidden
in the roll of netting that held up her pompadour."

He put it in Alice Cather's hand. She folded it back
the way it had been for years, without looking at it,
and handed it to Harry Cather. He struck a match,
held it to a corner of the paper and dropped it into
the fireplace.

"I was very young," Alice said evenly. "I was born
in Java, Colonel Primrose. My father was an Army
officer. He died of fever, and I got a job as governess
in a rich native family. It was a miserable life. Roy
Cather came along. I fell in love with him."

I suppose it was natural that I should have glanced up at where his portrait had been, over the mantel. And I started a little. It was there again. I hadn't noticed it when I came in with Colonel Primrose. I must have been staring at it open-mouthed, because it seemed an astounding thing to do, to put it back, now of all times.

Alice looked at me, a faint smile on her lips.

"I told you, Grace. It's not my husband—it's his brother. That's Harry's portrait. Roy Cather was my husband."

She looked at Harry for an instant, and turned to Colonel Primrose.

"I married him, as you realized. I didn't know he had a Japanese girl, and their child, living with him. He didn't bring them to our home until Mary was about to be born. When he did I was frantic. I didn't know what to do. Then Harry came out . . ."

"I brought her away with me, Colonel Primrose," Harry Cather said. "I couldn't let her stay. And we didn't intend to start this fiction we've lived under so long. The shipping people listed us as husband and wife, the Honolulu papers had it before we got here. It was simpler to let it go."

"Mary was born here," Alice said. "I hope she'll never have to know that Roy was her father. I'd rather die. All my life it's hung over me—he never let me forget it. Kumumato has always been our best friend. He knew, and whenever he saw him in Tokyo he'd try to get him to release me. And Roy always said come the war he might need a wife in Honolulu. There was nothing I could do that wouldn't become public here. I wouldn't have hesitated if he could have done any damage here. He wanted to stay here in the house. He gave me a list of the guests he wanted me to invite. I refused to do it. I think they had some idea that generals talk. I'm not sure that the life of a really important general or admiral would have been safe. And I truly thought he'd left, Colonel Primrose. Kumumato told me he had. A submarine was to pick him up."

"And what will you do now?" Colonel Primrose asked.

"It's something we've never considered ourselves in a position even to mention," Harry Cather said quietly. "We've both felt from the first that our only justification was keeping the strict letter of the law in our personal relationship, even after we both knew we had a deeper feeling for each other."

He looked over at Alice and smiled. "Or am I assuming too much?"

She smiled back at him and shook her head.

"We're going to marry as soon as possible," Harry Cather said. "On the Mainland."

Alice looked at Colonel Primrose. "Unless——"

Colonel Primrose shook his head with his quiet smile.

"It's not to the public interest to let people know Roy Cather came onto the Island. Not till after the war."

He was silent for a moment.

"The young sentry he killed died in the line of duty. Kumumato says Cather attacked him in the shelter. It was Cather's life or his. Interest is academic, on that point. As for Corinne . . . well, we'll have to let a jury decide."

When I went in to get my hat and bag to go down to the Pacific Club for lunch with Colonel Primrose, Mary was sitting on the foot of her bed pinning her short yellow curls up. She was in her bathing suit, her legs crossed under her.

"Close the door, Grace," she said.

I closed it and came in. She sat quietly the way she was, looking at herself in the mirror behind the dressing table.

"Swede says it doesn't matter, really," she said.

"What doesn't?" I asked.

"About who my father was."

She seemed a little surprised at my asking.

I said, "Oh."

"Didn't you hear Corinne call me 'Sister'? That's what she was telling Kumumato, down there, when he tried to make her stop. But I suppose I'd have found out sooner or later anyway. It's funny, Grace. I've often wondered why Mother and Dad have always had rooms at different ends of the house. They haven't acted like other people's parents. They never quarrelled or said horrid things to each other the way married people do. And I suppose they'll get married now, won't they?"

"I suppose so," I said.

She looked at herself steadily in the mirror for an instant.

"I don't feel any different. Swede says it doesn't make any difference."

"Of course not," I said. "Why should it?"

"I was worried last night. I thought maybe I'd wake up and find myself different. But I don't seem to be."

"I'd forget about it. I'd marry Swede and forget all about it."

She nodded. "That's what Swede says. But there's one thing—I don't want Mother ever to know I know. It's funny about these things, isn't it? Remember when we were going up the stairs and Corinne came down?"

I nodded.

"And she spoke to Kumumato—the first time?"

"Yes."

"She said, 'Greeting, my father that should have been.' That's when I began to get frightened. I didn't know the house servant Uncle Roy . . . my father married was Kumumato's wife until that instant. And I thought he was going to kill her then and there. It was the way he smiled. It really frightened me. Anyway, Mother mustn't ever know I know. You won't tell her?"

I shook my head. "Of course I won't, darling."

"Tommy and Dave know it. Corinne told them. They don't seem to think it's important either."

"It's not," I said.

She looked at me and smiled. "No, it really isn't," she said. "Well, Swede's waiting for me."

She got up. "I guess nobody has a right to be as happy as I am."

I heard a shout from the garden. She ran out onto the lanai, and I followed.

Swede, Tommy and Dave were down there in swimming trunks.

"Oh, dear," Mary said. She laughed. "Can't you get rid of them for a minute?"

"Take one, take all," said Lieutenant Thomas Edison Dawson cheerfully. "Are you coming, sister?"

They looked up at her, grinning. It was Swede who caught her when she jumped. He held her tight for a moment.

"Might as well get used to them," he said. "We're always going to have 'em underfoot."

"You can have an hour after lunch," Tommy said. "Here you are, lady.—David!"

Dave Boyer, grinning, produced from behind his back a large white spray of orchids from her own bank.

"Orchids for the bride," he said.

Tommy kissed her on the cheek. "You're a nice gal, Mary," he said. "We're proud to have you in the Organization."

Colonel Primrose was still in the house when I went out to the car. Had I known my friend Sergeant Phineas T. Buck would have been out there, I no doubt would have waited inside. He put his hand up in a very punctilious salute and opened the door for me. I got in.

Sergeant Buck cleared his throat.

"—You shouldn't ought to have done what you done, ma'am," he said, out of the corner of his mouth of course, and with a kind of menacing reproachfulness, and to my great surprise. "You shouldn't of turned him down, irregardless. He's lower than a snake's belly. Think you could reconsider, ma'am?"

Then he did turn that deep brassy red. It was as startling as it would be to hear a concrete mixer churning away and find milk and honey coming out.

Colonel Primrose was at the door.

"No offense meant, ma'am," Sergeant Buck said hastily.

"And none taken, Sergeant," I said.

We were all back where we started—except that I still didn't like being called a half-wit.

"O.K., sir," Sergeant Buck said.

"O.K.," Colonel Primrose answered.

He smiled at me as he sat down beside me. Sergeant Buck turned his head and spat accurately over into the grass at the side of the coral driveway. It was an odd kind of benediction, but there it was. He got in under the wheel. It was raining on the Pali road as we went out of the gate, but below us the city by the sea was brilliant and lovely, as clear and cool as crystal, a fortress of honor in a paradise where a brief moment of treachery was forever wiped out in the eternal setting of the yellow son of heaven.

CPSIA information can be obtained
at www.ICGtesting.com
Printed in the USA
LVHW091004090719
623548LV00001B/35/P